"Trying to be a gentleman, Ramsey?"

Fernando was about to stand, when he heard her question and the way she addressed him. "I don't have to try with you. It comes easy."

Contessa laughed. "Smooth," she said, complimenting him.

Fernando stood and favored her with a smirk. "I hope one day you'll take it as honesty."

Her desire to tease draining away, Contessa stood and let him help her into her coat. She watched him closely as he buttoned the stylish trench, secured the belt at her waist and tugged the fur collar around her ears.

"I'm not sleeping with you," she said once he was done.

Fernando kept his hands secure around the fur collar. "Do you think that's what a man wants if he's being nice to you?"

"It usually is."

"Well I'm not the usual."

That's what  ntly, as she let him into the chilly Chica

Books by AlTonya Washington

Kimani Romance

A Lover's Pretense
A Lover's Mask

Kimani Arabesque

Remember Love
Guarded Love
Finding Love Again
Love Scheme
A Lover's Dream

ALTONYA WASHINGTON

is a South Carolina native and 1994 graduate of Winston Salem State University in North Carolina. Her first contemporary novel, *Remember Love* (BET/Arabesque 2003), was nominated by *Romantic Times BOOKreviews* as Best First Multicultural Romance. Her novel *Finding Love Again* won the *Romantic Times BOOKreviews* Reviewer's Choice Award for Best Multicultural Romance 2004. Her fourth novel, *Love Scheme,* was nominated as Favorite Steamy Novel for the prestigious EMMA Award of Romance Slam Jam. She presently resides in North Carolina, where she works as a senior library assistant. *A Lover's Mask* is her ninth novel.

A LOVER'S
Mask

ALTONYA
WASHINGTON

KIMANI
ROMANCE

To the fabulous ladies and gents of the
"LoveAlTonya" Web group. Thanks guys for embracing
all the love and all the madness of the Ramsey family

 KIMANI PRESS™

ISBN-13: 978-0-373-86010-4
ISBN-10:   0-373-86010-2

A LOVER'S MASK

Copyright © 2007 by AlTonya Washington

www.kimanipress.com

Printed in U.S.A.

Dear Reader,

The way you've welcomed the Ramseys means more to me than you could possibly know. I had no idea that my desire to create a family series, mixing romance, mystery and drama, would be so enjoyed, and I thank you so very much.

I hope you found Fernando and Contessa's story— *A Lover's Mask,* the third book in the Ramsey family series—to be as passionate as it was revealing. I'm sure I answered some of your questions, even though I'm just as sure this story has raised new questions. Never fear, the next book in the series is ready and waiting. In the next episode, you'll discover what really happened the night of Sera Black's murder, and you'll discover *why* it happened.

Thanks for supporting me, guys! Please visit my Web site and join the LoveAlTonya Web group to keep up on all the latest Ramsey news!

Be blessed,

AlTonya
www.lovealtonya.com

Prologue

Seattle, Washington

A brisk wind blew, adding an even deeper chill to the overcast midmorning air. The Ramsey jets had just landed, following the return trip from Banff, Canada, where the family had just celebrated the completion of another Ramsey Group real estate project. As they departed the jets, some of the passengers were solemn, regarding the terrible scene at dinner the night before. Others appeared weary or just downright wary. The dinner was supposed to be a celebration to announce the engagement of

Quaysar Ramsey and his longtime love Tykira
Lowery. The gathering, however, was marred by the
appearance of Wake Robinson. Wake, an old friend
of Quaysar's, chose to pay an unexpected visit and
revealed various pieces of information regarding the
night of Sera Black's death. The murder of the teen
had haunted the family for decades. Needless to say,
Wake's appearance had cast a sour element to the
event. The exquisite trip to Banff, the successful
completion of the project and even the beautiful engagement announcement had been irrevocably
marred.

For Chicago publisher Contessa Warren it was her
top author and best friend Michaela Ramsey's discovery that one of the elder Ramseys was responsible for young Sera Black's death. Another thing
that weighed on County was knowing how Mick's
discovery was affecting her health. At least Quay and
Ty looked happy, County thought. She smiled,
watching the newly engaged couple embracing
where they leaned against one of the limos on hand
to take the group back to their various destinations.

County smoothed her hands across the sleeves of
the aubergine wool angora jacket and shook her
head. She supposed love and happiness could battle
the ugliness of the world if it was strong enough. Her
smile faded a little and she acknowledged that she
really wouldn't know. Love and happiness hadn't
seen fit as yet to pay her a visit.

Clearing her throat, Contessa focused on her friend Mick and her husband, Quest Ramsey. Ahh… more love and happiness, she noted and smiled again. If anyone deserved to be happy it was her best friend.

Mick stopped next to County where she stood near the limo's open door. "How long can you stay?" she asked, her eyes filling with apprehension.

County patted her cheek. "Only a few days and no more," she added when Mick opened her mouth to argue. "You need to focus on resting and the baby and not cackling with me or worrying over any of this other mess."

Mick rolled her eyes and flicked a windblown curl from her cheek. "And I suppose you won't be coming down to Savannah for Quay and Ty's wedding, either?" she knowingly asked.

"Oh, honey I can't. I can just imagine the work that's waiting for me," County said in excuse, not about to tell her friend that she was in no mood to attend a wedding. "I'll be giving Quay and Ty my gift before I head back to Chicago," she said.

Mick sighed defeatedly and accepted that County's mind was made up. Looking back at Quest, she gave a slight nod and let him get her settled in the back of the car.

"Is she going to be all right?" County asked Quest when he'd gotten his wife comfortable.

Quest nodded, though his haunting black and

gray eyes harbored concern. "She'll be fine," he said
and patted County's hand to assure her. "I already
put in a call to her OB. He's about to put her on bed
rest for a few weeks."

"Good," County said and nodded her satisfaction.

Quest squeezed her wrist one last time, and then
looked out over the landing strip. "We'll be ready to
pull out in about ten minutes," he said.

County nodded, watching Quest walk off to speak
with his twin brother Quaysar. She leaned against the
limo, letting the brisk wind hit her face a second or
two longer. She was about to join Mick when she felt
a hand cup her elbow. Turning, her lips parted as she
looked way up to find Fernando Ramsey at her side.

"Mr. Ramsey," she greeted, her luminous brown
eyes narrowing a bit as she studied his incredible
features.

"She all right?" Fernando inquired of his cousin's
wife while nodding toward the limo's interior.

County glanced across her shoulder. "I think so.
Quest says her doctor may put her on a few weeks
bed rest."

Fernando's translucent brown gaze became fixed
on County's face then. "Will you be staying with
them?" he asked.

"Only for a few days. Then it's back to Chicago
and work. Two things I've missed way too much of."

"Hmph, yeah the world of the Ramseys can be
a bit much."

County's brows rose a notch. "Hmph, a bit."

"Would you have a cup of coffee with me before you leave?"

County wondered if any other man could make a simple request for coffee sound like a request for seduction. She shivered beneath her quarter length jacket as though her spine had been kissed by a freezing breeze. "Didn't I cut you down enough on the plane?" she asked, after ordering herself to calm down.

Fernando smiled and Contessa found herself returning the sentiment in reaction to the way his mesmerizing eyes crinkled at the corners.

"Obviously I survived," he surmised.

County smoothed one hand across the sleeve of her jacket. "Whatever would we talk about?" she playfully sighed. "Somehow I don't think your family is the most fun topic."

Fernando bowed his head and County took a moment to admire the crop of gorgeous rich brown curls he possessed.

"I think we could come up with quite a few fun things to talk about," he predicted.

"And you won't take no for an answer?" she guessed.

Broad shoulders rose in a slow shrug as Fernando stepped closer. "I'll take no if I really, really have to. But I really, *really* don't want to," he admitted, easing massive hands into the pockets of his black overcoat. "Besides, I may never see you again and I'd regret not asking you to come with me forever."

Lord, did all the Ramseys have such a way with words? County thought, shocked by a stab of something scandalous that stirred someplace unmentionable.

Again, he stepped closer. "Well?" he taunted.

The scent of his cologne enveloped her and County swallowed as though the action would do something to diminish it. This man was beautifully overwhelming and so very tempting. What harm could talking do?

"Just let me say goodbye to Mick," she decided, watching as he strolled away. Shaking her head, she bent into the car and snapped her fingers to get Michaela's attention. "I'm gonna come to the house later, okay?"

"Why? What's wrong?" Mick wanted to know, a frown already marring her brow.

"Nothing, nothing. The trip was just so intense and the day is so refreshing. I guess I want to be out in it a little longer before heading inside," she explained coolly.

"You're sure you're okay? Do we need to get another car for you?"

"Mick, Mick, I'm fine. Stop worrying," County urged, leaning close to plant a kiss to her friend's cheek. "I'll be to the house in a couple of hours. I promise."

"Okay…well, be careful," Mick ordered, and then handed Contessa her purse from the opposite seat.

County accepted the purse, blew a kiss to Mick and stood. She took in the sight of Fernando standing a few feet away. Careful? Ha! That word and *that* man were clearly a mismatch, but she was far too intrigued to turn back.

Chapter 1

Chicago—New Years Eve

Contessa realized she was going to have to make her great escape from this party and soon. She'd just used her last excuse not to dance or engage in conversation that would only give one of the many available men there the idea that he'd be leaving with her for the evening. She cursed herself for even accepting the invite to the New Year's bash, but it *was* New Year's.

It was New Year's Eve and she was alone and it was by choice. And it scared the hell out of her.

She'd thought of calling and sharing her woes with Michaela, but knew her best friend was busy with her husband on the special evening. Her husband. Mick being married had put so much in perspective for her. Contessa found herself sick with fear that she'd wind up an old maid with a house full of cats. Or dogs. Or cats *and* dogs.

"Dammit why am I doing this to myself *now?*" she raged, looking down to her lap as she hissed the question. *This is stupid, County. That life isn't for you. You know that.* Then why was she finding herself wishing for it more and more over the last couple of years?

Suddenly, she blinked, tilting her head to get a better look at what had caught her eye across the crowded dining area.

What in the world is he doing here? County silently inquired.

From her spot at her favorite corner table she could see that she had a perfect view—stress on the word *perfect.* Much as it unnerved her to admit, he'd occupied a great portion of her thoughts since the Banff trip. Actually, it was the drinks they'd shared afterward and the conversation that went along. It felt too good to vent, she remembered. They spoke of Mick, and County voiced her concerns over wanting her best friend to rest and how the case was just becoming more and more complex.

Conversation wasn't forced or uncomfortable. It

flowed. They discussed, they debated, they bantered and the only reason they parted company after three hours was because Mick called worried and wondering when she was coming home. Contessa had always believed she preferred her men leanly muscular, not blatantly massive and powerful. Fernando Ramsey, however, was precisely that.

The caramel toned devil in her sights now was that and more. Besides, she'd always reasoned a man who worked so hard to maintain upper body power usually lost out on something in more important areas, right? Of course, she wasn't one to speculate. Should the opportunity ever present itself for more…verification, she thought she'd be quite willing to investigate.

She had, however, taken the opportunity to evaluate the man during their time together after the Banff trip. A brief time, but enough for her to agree that he was indeed a delicious thing. His skin was flawless—rare for a man to have such perfect skin. Her time around the Ramsey men, though, had told her whatever interior imperfections they might possess, it was impossible to judge by outward appearances.

As most of the men in his family were dark, Fernando was a rich caramel shade—as if he'd been drenched in the stuff. Everything about him was large and cool, from the mesmerizing shade of his deep-set eyes to the close cut beard of dark brown that added a certain roughish element to his face. Unconsciously, County rubbed her fingers together and imagined what it might feel like to bury them in the silky close cut curls covering his head.

Closing her eyes, County told herself she was getting carried away. This lack of sex, companionship or whatever was really starting to get to her. Of course, she was always careful in her choice of men and not nearly as fancy-free as her best friend Mick may have believed. Still, she'd had her share of encounters. Sadly, true commitment continued to elude her. County couldn't help but wonder if that was the fault of the man or herself.

What the hell? She finally decided, brows rising a few notches as she continued to regard Fernando. It couldn't hurt to send a bottle of champagne to his table. After all, it *was* New Year's. Besides, she had the feeling he'd want to keep the drinks coming judging from the looks of his two female companions who'd already finished off one bottle of wine and were at work on a second.

Trailing petal pink manicured nails across her bare arms, she again wondered what he was doing there. Chicago was a bit removed from his Seattle stomping ground. She wondered if he knew her friend James Aston who owned the yacht restaurant where the celebration was being held.

"Ms. Warren? Are you all right over here?"

County smiled up at the waiter. "Actually, I'd like to send a bottle of champagne to that noisy table over there," she decided finally and cast an airy wave in the general direction.

The giggly, busty beauties at Fernando's table had grown consistently louder. The waiter had no confusion about to whom County was referring and nodded.

"This can't be Contessa Warren all by herself on New Year's Eve?"

County rolled her eyes when she heard the question voiced just a few seconds following the waiter's departure. Forcing a smile she looked up to see two more male acquaintances who had been successful in sniffing her out.

"It's me," she sang, clasping her hands together as Gayle Hubbard and Cory Preston joined her.

"All alone?" Cory asked, sounding as though he couldn't believe it.

County folded her arms across the sequined square bodice of the pink silk and chiffon spaghetti strapped tunic she wore. "Believe it Cory and I'd like to keep it that way," she shared pointedly.

"Ouch," Gayle replied, bristling as though her words cut deep. "Baby, don't start the year off this way. You're much too fine to be all alone on a night like this."

"Mmm, I know," County sighed, shaking her head when the two men chuckled. They launched a debate on which one of them was more worthy of her company for the remainder of the evening. Meanwhile, Contessa's attention and gaze returned to Fernando's table in time to see the waiter arriving there with the champagne.

Confusion registered on Fernando's handsome face, as the waiter motioned toward County's table. Fernando's gaze narrowed as he sought to get a better look at the woman with the two men across the room. He took in her honey toned skin bared by the elegant style of her outfit, the chic boyish cut she now sported and realization rushed forth.

Clearly, Fernando's two companions didn't care who sent the additional refreshment. They began to wiggle in their seats, clinking their glasses in anticipation of the bubbly delight.

At her table, Contessa reached for her handbag and the stylish peony burlap long coat. "'Scuse me, fellas," she said amidst their incessant discussion. Her thoughts wholly focused on the devastating Ramsey across the room, she took a stroll to the bar knowing he'd be by her side soon enough.

"When a man buys a woman a drink, it's usually because he'd like to join her. Does that hold true for women as well?"

County smiled at his question, feeling her flesh riddle with goose bumps in reaction to the warm depth of his voice. She turned, tilting her head back to study him as his eyes caressed her face before moving on to the generous swell of her bosom.

County followed the line of his gaze and then

looked up and nodded toward the two women he'd been with. "I thought your dates could use a bit more," she said.

Fernando responded with a slow nod and smile. "So you did it just for them?"

"And you too," County quickly added, her expression turning wicked. "I'm sure you want to keep them happy."

"And why is that?"

Again, County cast another suggestive look across the room. "Oh, I'd say you're gonna have the time of your life tonight."

"I'm beginning to think so too," Fernando agreed, still focused completely on her.

County tilted her head, not pretending to misread him in the least. "What about your dates?"

"That was business, not pleasure."

"And what am I?"

"Definitely not business."

County pushed one hand inside the pocket of her black moleskin trousers. "So you think I'm that sort of girl?" she asked in a challenging tone. "To go home with a man I hardly know?"

Fernando drew closer, practically shielding County's view of the room with his massive build. She studied the breadth of his shoulders beneath the gorgeous fabric of his navy wool boucle textured suit coat and wondered if all that size really belonged to him.

"We can talk all night, but in the morning you're mine," he spoke just loudly enough for her to hear.

Contessa shut out the voice that sang, "danger, danger" and cleared her throat softly. "Does that line usually work?"

Fernando grinned, leaning closer still to retrieve her coat from the bar. "I've never used it before," he admitted. "I suppose we'll find out in the morning."

Contessa prayed he couldn't hear her breathing and told the singing voice to shut up. She let him help her into her coat, then curved her fingers into the crook of the arm he offered. She prayed again that he didn't hear the low moan she uttered at the feel of the rock solid biceps that flexed ever so gently. *Hell, it's New Year's,* she reasoned. Together, they left the yacht.

One week later...

"I know Jay pulled out all the stops," Mick guessed when she and County spoke by phone one January afternoon.

"He did at that."

Contessa's unenthusiastic response earned a raised eyebrow from Mick. Her curiosity roused and then her suspicion.

"It was a party on a boat and not a very good one," County remarked when Mick remained silent. "Jay's losing his touch," she added nastily in reference to their friend James Aston. "I left before the balloons fell" she saw fit to share.

Mick got more comfortable in the lounge she occupied and smiled at County's rambling—very uncharacteristic. "Mmm, you say you left before the balloons fell, eh? Alone?"

"Dammit, now what's that supposed to mean?" County snapped.

Mick let silence carry the conversation for almost twenty seconds. "Jeez, it's me who's pregnant. I thought *I* was suppose to be the touchy one."

"I'm not touchy."

"I disagree. Your New Year's must've been a bust."

"Hell, Mick, what's your hang-up with New Year's all of a sudden?"

"It *is* usual conversation for supposed friends who haven't talked since *before* the holidays," Mick retorted, her own temper beginning to simmer.

"The holidays," County sniffed indignantly. "Holidays are for families. You have Quest and—"

"You're *still* my family," Mick interrupted, shaking her head when she heard Contessa sigh over the line. "I'm surprised to be doing all of the talking anyway. You usually have my head spinning with one of your scandalous tales of an all night romp with one of your—"

"Damn, you must really think I'm a slut," County hissed, massaging the tension that had suddenly formed in her neck.

Mick was unnerved, having heard the subtle change in her friend's voice. Again, she let silence take control. "I'm sorry, Contessa. I'm truly sorry," she swore.

County rolled her eyes, knowing the last thing she wanted to do was upset her pregnant friend. "Listen, it's just business aggravations and *I'm* the one who should be apologizing."

"Do you want to talk about it?" Mick asked, not believing for a minute that business woes were at the root of County's mood.

"Nooo, I don't want to talk about it. It's petty."

"And I'm worried about you."

"Aw Mick, come on. You know how we do. Don't start getting sappy on me now. You always tease me and I love it."

"Yeah, but there comes a time when a joke isn't funny anymore and I *am* sorry."

"Accepted," County replied, praying that was the end of it. "It's all right Mick. I'm good.

Far from convinced, Mick decided to stop pressing. "Just come to me if you need to."

"I promise," County said, crossing her fingers as she uttered the lie.

"Now, about my baby shower." Mick switched conversations and sat a little straighter on the lounge.

"You're scandalous," County criticized. "Planning your own damn shower. Other people are suppose to do that for you, you know?"

Mick rolled her eyes. "Please, I want this done my way since this will be my only child and therefore my *only* shower."

"Your *only* child?" County parroted, more than a little stunned. "Does Quest know this?"

"Please County," Mick whispered, her tone solemn, "you know I'll be lucky to even do a *halfway* decent job with this baby. I don't think it'd be wise to test the waters more than once, you know?"

"Michaela, please don't make a decision like this based on your own childhood."

Mick couldn't manage a response.

"So when is this shower?" County asked, hoping to lighten the mood.

"March, if I can move by then," Mick said, curls falling across her eyes when she looked down at her ever-increasing tummy. "I'll be six months by then."

"Ha! Six months and the size of a baby whale," County teased.

"Anyway, just make sure your butt is out here two weeks early. I wanna spend some time with you. Just us."

"Aw Mick, girl, do you really need me out there that long?" County whined.

"Please," Mick said. "You have a million-dollar, independent publishing house that practically runs itself, so don't even try it. Besides, I miss you."

County raked her fingers across her short cut and smiled. "I miss you too."

"So?"

"So I'll be there in Seattle two weeks early."

"Good. Now I'm hanging up before you find another reason to back out. I love you."

"Love you too," County returned, sending Mick a kiss through the receiver before clicking off the phone.

Leaning back in the vanilla suede chair behind her glass desk, she closed her eyes and tried to block out how much she really missed her dear friend. *I could really use your advice now, Mick,* she admitted silently. Alas, Mick was finally happy with a man who cherished her. Now they were going to have a child together. The last thing County wanted was to give her worries. Besides, County was sure that what she was going through was only a phase. She'd be thirty-four next year and it was just the chiming of her biological clock. Yeah, that had to be it.

Moderately satisfied by the assumption, County sighed and nodded. Tugging on the cuffs of her gray tweed suit coat, she sat straight and prepared to tackle another day's chores at the office. She was settling in to read another proposal from the conglomerate that had been salivating to buy her publishing house, when a knock sounded on her office door.

"Hey," County greeted, watching her head editor Spivey Freeman and Jenean Rays head of the fact checking department arrive with serious expressions.

Groaning, County let her head fall back against her chair. "Not now guys," she pleaded, knowing what they wanted to discuss: the unfinished Ramsey novel.

"County, we've been more than patient," Spivey argued, his high brow worn with frown lines.

"That's right Contessa. You've gotta make a decision sometime." Jenean added.

"We've been damned lucky someone else hasn't already jumped on this thing," Spivey cited.

"You're right," County admitted, surprised as well that a Ramsey novel hadn't already beat the Contessa House version to the shelves. Spivey made a valid point and even she couldn't deny the novel would be more engrossing in light of the fact that the killer had been caught—more or less.

Spivey and Jenean watched their boss expectantly, waiting on some tilt of her head or wave of her hand to signify the go-ahead.

"What about the rest of the family?" County asked, idly studying the spiked heel of one of the black leather boots she wore. "There's more to the Ramseys' story than what happened to Sera Black," she reminded them.

In response, Spivey hefted the three accordion folders he'd brought into the office. The folders teemed with so much information, they had to be secured with several fat rubber bands.

"All the data collected on every member of the Ramseys," Spivey announced.

"Every member?" County asked, her thoughts turning immediately to Fernando Ramsey.

"Even though formal charges have never been filed, there are some pretty brow raising facts in that mountain of stuff," Jenean shared, entwining a heavy braid between her fingers. "We've got the makings of one hell of a book," she predicted.

"Maybe two even," Spivey mused.

"Is the research complete?" County inquired, rearing back in her chair while considering their news. "Are we really ready to go forward with this? Do you guys have an author in mind to work on the draft, or at the very least an outline?"

"There's still work to be done," Spivey admitted, exchanging a glance with Jenean.

"There're a lot of Ramseys. All of them with interesting backgrounds," Jenean cautioned.

County agreed. "So how long would it take to complete the research if I give the go-ahead to continue? Well?" she prompted, when the two remained silent.

"That's hard to pinpoint County," Spivey acknowledged. "We're successful, but we're still a small house. It'd take the efforts of almost everyone on staff to wade through the information we do have."

"But the rewards of such hard work would be astronomical," Jenean guaranteed.

County knew it was true. In spite of the house being such a financial success, it still lacked name recognition. She wanted Contessa House to be on the lips of the most discriminating personalities in the literary world. After all, her business was all she had. Her resolve in place, County stood and fixed Spivey and Jenean with challenging looks. "All right, get on it. Get on it. Get everyone you can spare on it and we'll talk again next week."

Spivey and Jenean almost tripped over themselves when the decision reached their ears. They rambled nonstop on their way out the door. Alone in her office again, County hugged herself and then turned to judge the view of downtown from her tenth story window.

Chicago in winter was no joke. The wind whipped without mercy. Snow blanketed the streets and then revisited with even more of its icy white for days to come. County shook her head, watching a crew of city workers preparing for that weekend's expected storm. The group set up sturdy ropes along the sidewalks to assist pedestrians who had to travel the treacherous area by foot.

"Dammit," County hissed, suddenly remembering the lunch appointment she was about to be late for. Glancing repeatedly at her watch, she grabbed a heavy black double breasted trench from the sofa and raced out the office.

Marvin's was a high profile neighborhood club located a few blocks from Contessa House. County had received her weekly call from Dark Squires Enterprises requesting another meeting. The two men she usually met with were so kind and persuasive, County often hated turning them down. Still, they tried.

Unfortunately, for the Dark Squires partners, today she was in no mood to coddle men no matter how sweet and charming they were. It was freezing, she was aggravated and she was starving.

"This is what makes working here worth all the headache."

County forgot her frustration the moment she stepped past the restaurant's double maple doors. The proprietor's nephews, Sam and Charles, greeted her with their usual tease.

"The two of you say that to all us old ladies," County voiced her usual reply and accepted her hug and kiss on the cheek from the tall nineteen-year-old brothers who worked their uncle's shop during their college breaks. "Isn't it a bit late, though?" she inquired, once Charles released her, "shouldn't you guys be back at school?"

Sam's and Charles' expressions mirrored unease. "Uncle Les is pretty bad, so we're overseeing things until he's better," Charles said.

As Lester Marvin was a staple in the area, the news of his lingering illness hit County deeply. She could tell from the looks on the boys' faces that the man's recovery was not expected.

"We're gonna transfer our credits to finish school instead of going back to D.C.," Sam explained.

"I'll be sure to visit Mr. Les this weekend," County promised. "I want you two to call if you need anything, all right?" She waited for their nods. Standing on her toes, she favored them both with a sweet kiss to the jaw.

The handsome teens escorted Contessa to the table where her lunch companions waited. Meanwhile, Fernando Ramsey followed her movement across the dining room. He was mildly surprised to feel his hand curve into a fist as he watched the tender moment she shared with her escorts. Young— *too* young, he decided, as a smirk curved his mouth. Of course, he realized women who looked like Contessa Warren had their pick of anyone at anytime.

It was more than looks with her, though, he acknowledged, and watched as she took her place at the table. The woman exuded something—a silken tether that beckoned a man to simply reach out and take hold to the promise of supreme pleasure that awaited with her.

Come off it Fern, he told himself. She was just a woman. *More than a woman,* something forced him to admit. Fernando leaned back against the booth he occupied. He shook his head as his thoughts took him back to New Year's Eve. Regardless of how impromptu that night or the day after had been, something had happened. She'd done something— affected some part of his psyche.

Taking great pleasure in the arms of a woman was about as natural for him as breathing. The next day, the event was a distant memory. But not with Contessa. She matched him sexually yes—oh, hell, yes. But her wit and verbal banter seemed to arouse him just as easily. Sure she'd probably slap his face if he told her he'd very much like to see her *and* sleep with her again. In spite of her allure and confidence, he got the impression one-night stands weren't the norm for her. Besides, after their seventh round of lovemaking on New Year's Day, she as much as told him it would never happen again. She seemed to hate saying it as much as he hated hearing it.

Fernando was willing to bet good money that Contessa Warren wasn't a woman who reversed her decisions once they were made. Damn.

Somewhere in the distance he heard his name being called. With an indecipherable grunt of regret, he realized it was his two lunch companions. He'd completely forgotten they were seated right next to him.

County had called them his dates and who wouldn't think such a thing? The leggy, voluptuous adult film beauties were about to grace the pages of one of his magazines and every man envied the liking they'd taken to him. Fernando wouldn't deny it. He knew if he hadn't seen County on New Year's Eve, winding up in the middle of a lusty sandwich was a definite possibility.

Now, however, their advances, light caressing and

the brushes of their enhanced cleavage against his arms and back were grating on his nerves.

"Fernie, are you all right?" asked one of the beauties, while trailing a nail in his beard.

"I'm good. Look," he began, straightening in the seat and forcing the ladies to give him space, "everything here is a go. We've negotiated a favorable deal with your agents and your studio, so my part in this arrangement is done," he said, waving toward his driver who waited at the bar. "James can take you back to your hotel or wherever you wish to go," he told them once the man stood near the table.

"Ladies," James prompted, with a wave of his hand to urge them from their seats.

The beauties pouted, but knew it'd be unwise and pointless to argue with Fernando. Instead, they kissed his cheek and said their goodbyes. Fernando cast a knowing wink at James and polished off the rest of his drink to celebrate their departure. Angling his massive form to a more comfortable position within the booth, he enjoyed the peace and watched Contessa.

"Guys, I was surprised to be hearing from you so soon after our meeting before Christmas," County said once she'd greeted her lunch dates.

"We received permission to increase our offer on the house," Anson Carter announced as his partner, Graham Johnson nodded. "We didn't want to waste time in presenting it to you. We're sure you'll have a change of heart."

County shook her head and smiled. "Well guys, I *am* impressed by your tenacity. But, as usual, I'm afraid you'll be leaving empty-handed again."

"Ms. Warren, do you understand that we can make you a very wealthy woman?" Anson said, as though he were sharing some guarded secret.

County smiled, watching her French tipped nails tapping against the silverware. "Boys do *you* understand that I'm already a very wealthy woman?"

"We can make you wealthier." Graham pointed out.

"I'm hoping that's what my business will do for me."

"It can!"

"You both know what I mean," County said, chuckling when they spoke in unison. She watched the looks on their handsome dark faces cloud as they silently struggled to come up with a way to convince her. "Don't bother," she said, when Anson opened his mouth. "My mind's made up," she added.

"But—"

"My decision is firm and won't change," she guaranteed, waving towards a waiter in the distance.

Meanwhile, Anson and Graham looked lost— almost unnerved. Clearly, they didn't want to return to the office empty-handed.

"Whiskey—" County ordered from the waiter once he arrived at the table.

Suddenly, Graham nudged Anson's arm and nodded.

"We're sorry we can't do business Ms. Warren," Anson said, as he and his partner stood.

"Please enjoy your lunch on us," Graham offered.

County nodded, grateful for an end to the meeting and hoping her eyes weren't sparkling too much in anticipation of their leaving. Still, she was surprised to find them giving up so easily—something they rarely did.

"You guys have a good afternoon," she said, already reaching for a menu.

"Will you be having lunch with us today, Ms. Warren?" The waiter asked when he returned with Contessa's drink shortly after Graham and Anson's departure.

"I think I will," County decided, sipping her drink as she perused the menu.

"I'll just give you a few moments," the waiter said, "would you like a refill on your drink Mr. Ramsey?" he inquired, stepping past County.

Seeing Fernando standing next to the table as though there were nothing out of the ordinary about it, rendered County motionless. At last, she was able to lean back in her chair and observe him with a soft smile gracing her mouth.

"It'll take a menu," he decided, nodding when the waiter set off to get him one.

County watched him choose a seat and waited for him to tell her what he was doing there.

"Are you alone?" he asked, resting his elbows on either arm of the deep chair.

"Would it matter?" County responded, her brown eyes narrowed in challenge.

Fernando shook his head and resituated his massive frame in the chair.

"Are *you* alone?" she asked.

"Would it matter?" he returned.

County chuckled. "Touché," she conceded. "I'd just feel really bad about taking you away from your dates twice in one month."

"Well, technically, it was *last* month that you took me away from them."

County tapped one nail to her chin while considering the clarification. "You're right," she said upon remembering. "To hell with 'em."

Fernando massaged his bearded cheek and fixed her with a suspicious look. "What made you think I was with them, anyway?" he wanted to know.

"That's right," County sighed, her oval honey toned face a picture of realization, "you probably never see the same woman after one date."

"You wound me, County," his deep voice cooed.

"Then again," she went on, dismissing the soothing tone of his baritone voice, "perhaps you haven't…consummated the date?" she lightly probed.

Fernando tugged on the cuff of his jacket and shrugged. "A gentleman never tells."

The waiter returned with refills on both Fernando's and Countessa's drinks, along with a menu for Fernando. "Are we ready to order?" he asked County.

"Oh, I haven't even had time to look," she said with a start.

"Too busy giving me a hard time," Fernando shared, earning a wicked smile from County.

"I'll give you two more time," the waiter decided before leaving them alone again.

"So, about my supposed *dates*. They really are business I swear."

"Tsk, tsk, tsk. You're far too gorgeous to have to pay for it."

Fernando blinked and tilted his head in curiosity. "Are you complimenting me?"

"Of course I am," she coolly admitted, her expressive gaze still trained on the menu. "Hasn't a woman ever told you that?"

Fernando barely raised his hand in a flip wave. "In her own way."

County set aside her menu. "What way? By gazing longingly into your eyes while she bats her lashes and laughs at every witty or *un*witty remark you make?"

Fernando shifted in his chair, feeling the front of his trousers grow snug as the twinges of arousal began to swell his manhood. Oral banter courtesy of Contessa Warren was as good as oral sex, he decided then and there. Clearing his throat, he concentrated on focusing his thoughts on something completely nonerotic.

"I'm sorry," County whispered, pressing her hand across the black V-neck jersey blouse she wore beneath her suit, "we were discussing your dates who are actually business."

"They actually are," Fernando confirmed, the sensual curve of his mouth twitched against the need to laugh.

"So you're *not* paying them?"

"No. Well, yes. Technically."

County laughed loud and unashamed. "*That* you'll have to explain."

"They're working for me."

"Ha! I'll bet they are."

The waiter returned amidst boisterous laughter and immediately asked if he should return later.

"I think it'll be a while before we get around to eating," County predicted. "Mr. Ramsey's got some explaining to do. But you can bring me another whiskey and I have a feeling the gentleman could use several more drinks."

"I'll keep the beverages coming," the waiter promised, close to laughter himself.

"Now, where were we?" County asked Fernando, her vibrant stare made even more vibrant in the presence of cunning.

For a moment, he could only stare at her. He

enjoyed everything he saw on the outside—and inside. This was a woman who could match him and he honestly thought the only women who existed were either sickeningly sweet and over accommodating, too eager to please or devious, conniving, self-serving and ready to betray.

Contessa Warren...Contessa...she was something else. He'd come to the realization long ago. His gut had never betrayed him and it was now telling him to hold on to her—to not let her too far out of his sight for too long. This was a woman to keep—a woman who could be a powerful, completely satisfying partner in bed, in business, in life.

County was snapping her fingers before his face and chuckling when he blinked. "Have you created your lie—excuse me, *explanation* yet?"

"The girls really are business," he swore, nodding when the waiter placed refills on the table. "They're going to be featured in one of my magazines."

"Mmm...the plot thickens," County said, leaning back in her chair. "I wouldn't have pegged you for a literary man."

"Too gorgeous, right?" he probed, chuckling when County sent him a saucy wink.

"Well, something tells me those two aren't gracing the pages of a happy homemaker magazine," she said.

"Not quite. I own several magazines," he told her, taking a deep drink from his glass. "Two I run from here in Chicago. Those two will be featured in one of my, um…gentleman's magazines."

"Well, I must say I've never met a man with so many interesting…interests." County admitted, her eyes brightening as she was thoroughly intrigued.

"Then why not see them firsthand? Join me tomorrow for a tour of my offices?"

"A tour?" County laughed, shaking her head. "That really isn't necessary. I believe you."

"I really want you to see the place."

"Why?"

"Maybe I'm trying to impress you."

"You've done that already."

Fernando bowed his head, acknowledging the suggestive meaning of her words. "I don't want you to think I'm a one-dimensional guy."

County smoothed one hand across her chic cut. "Oh, I don't think that. Trust me."

Fernando's warm deep-set gaze seemed to intensify. "I'm being serious," he said in a mildly warning tone.

County shrugged one shoulder. "So am I."

"Is this a date or not?" he asked.

"Hmm," County closed her eyes, tugging her bottom lip between her teeth. "Yes."

Fernando thought the word had never sounded sweeter.

Chapter 2

County and Fernando placed their orders after the waiter's fifth journey to their table. Several quiet moments passed as they dined on delicious curry chicken with rice, spinach salads and hot, buttery rolls.

"So is there any particular reason why you live in Seattle yet run your business from Chicago?" County asked, stabbing a spinach leaf with her fork.

"I only run two magazines from Chicago," Fernando clarified. "I thought about relocating here while I was getting the pubs established. I decided against it."

"Why?"

"Because my last name is Ramsey."

"Ah…" County sighed, forgetting her food for a moment. "Trying to be your own man?"

Fernando's grin sparked the adorable crinkles at the corners of his eyes. "I was already my own man. I just didn't want anyone to know I was Marcus Ramsey's son. But I'll be damned if he hadn't already made a name for himself here, too."

"So the bulk of your empire is in Seattle?" County surmised in a teasing manner, feeling the chill in his voice when he spoke of his father.

"That's right. I only have the two magazines here," he confirmed.

"So what else are you involved in?" she asked, returning her attention to the succulent curry chicken. "It's not for my files," she said when he seemed reluctant to respond, "I already have plenty of info on you."

"Is that right?" Fernando said while leaning back to regard her. "Now it's your turn to elaborate."

"Well, there's your colorful childhood for starters," County began, realizing that he'd shifted the subject but deciding to play along anyway, "a tour of duty in reform school and then it was on to the big house."

"You're thorough," Fernando commended.

County shrugged. "I try. You know, you should become a motivational speaker. 'How to turn your life around or become a *legal* crook,'" she joked.

Again, Fernando placed a hand across his heart. "You continue to wound me," he lamented.

"So what would possess someone like you to get into trouble?"

"Someone like me?" Fernando parroted, toying with his earlobe as he spoke. "What? You mean someone with money and no problems?"

County smiled knowingly and silently conceded his point with a nod.

"Contessa, a kid with money is a kid with absentee parents."

"Not always," County argued.

"But many times."

"So your father didn't have time for you or your brothers?"

"Oh, he had time, but there's a difference between having time and *making* time."

In spite of the deep unwavering strength behind his voice, County could tell there was still hurt within him. "What about your mother?" she asked.

"Phenomenal," Fernando spoke without hesitation, admiration filling his captivating eyes momentarily. "But a boy needs his father. To us, Marcus was just another man. Perhaps having him closer would've blinded us to what he was really like."

County recrossed her legs and leaned closer to the table. "But he's still your father—still in your lives…" she trailed away, watching his face tighten with some tense emotion.

"Not for long," he muttered.

She heard each word and could almost feel the

hate rolling from his tongue. It made him seem so different, so unapproachable. She certainly didn't care for the sinister element the emotion cast across his very handsome face. Finding herself at an uncharacteristic loss for words, she clasped her hands in her lap and remained silent.

"You in the mood for dessert?"

His question, returned some of the easiness to the table. County raised her hand as though she were about to testify.

"I couldn't eat another bite," she said, casting a look of concern towards the dining room's tall paned windows. "Besides, I think I've played it risky too long. That snow's gonna barrel down any second and my office is two blocks away."

"You intend to walk?" Fernando asked, his concern evident as a furrow formed between his long, sleek brows.

"Oh, it's fine. The walk isn't nearly as long as you think," County insisted.

"It's freezing out there."

"I'm used to it."

Fernando shook his head. "Not while I'm around, you're not," he decided and reached inside his suit coat to retrieve his wallet.

"Fernando—"

"Hush," he urged in the softest voice, dropping money to the table before clicking on his cell phone. "Hey, where are you?" he asked, pleased to hear that his driver James had dropped off the *dates* and was parked out in front of the restaurant. "We'll be right out."

"Trying to be a gentleman, Ramsey?"

Fernando was about to stand, when he heard her question and the way she addressed him. "I don't have to try with you. It comes easy."

County laughed. "Smooth," she complimented.

Fernando stood and favored her with a smirk. "I hope one day you'll take it as honesty."

Her desire to tease draining away, County stood and let him help her into her coat. She watched him closely as he buttoned the stylish trench, secured the belt at her waist and tugged the fur collar around her ears.

"I'm not sleeping with you," she said once he was done.

Fernando kept his hands secure around the fur collar. "Do you think that's what a man wants if he's being nice to you?"

"It usually is."

"Well, I'm not the usual."

That's what worries me, County remarked silently and then let him lead her out of the restaurant.

St. Croix, Virgin Islands

Tykira Lowery Ramsey stretched and smiled lazily when her husband rose from beneath the pool of ocean blue water.

"Now I see why you requested a suite with its own pool," she whispered, trailing her nails across his jaw.

Quay shrugged one shoulder. "Sometimes you gotta have privacy," he told his wife, grinning devilishly as he leaned in to kiss her.

Ty uttered a weak moan when she tasted her body on his mouth. Her moans increased in volume as she suckled his tongue in a desperate, lusty manner. She felt the familiar tingle grow in intensity as it trickled all the way to her toes and she became lost in his embrace.

"Time for bed," Quay announced when he pulled away after several moments.

"We just got out of bed," Ty said amidst her laughter.

"Damn, why'd we do that?"

Ty smiled at her husband, pretended to be confused and followed suit. "Hmm? Let me think…" she sighed, and then snapped her fingers, "because we wanted to make love in the pool."

"Right," Quay drawled, filling his palms with her breasts and preparing to feast.

"Quay, Quay wait," Ty lightly protested.

Of course, he didn't listen. "This is what newly-weds do on their honeymoon," he said, suckling madly on a firm nipple.

"I know," Ty gasped, cupping his neck and arching more of herself into his mouth. "Mmm…but we've been on our honeymoon going on two months…"

Quay sobered, his dark eyes narrowing as he moved back to study her face. "Aren't you having a good time?"

Ty splashed water in his face. "Don't ask foolish questions," she said, kissing his cheek when he smiled.

"Well, what's wrong here? Why are you telling me to stop?" he asked, looking longingly at her breasts as if she'd hurt his feelings.

"Actually baby, I was hoping you could tell me."

"Huh?"

Ty looked up at the gorgeous late afternoon sky and braced herself. "Well…it's just that you haven't called anyone in Washington or even checked in on the business."

"I talked to Q a week ago. Everything's fine."

"But don't you want to see for yourself?"

Quay braced his hands on the pool on either side of Ty. "You *did* say you were having a good time, right?"

"Just how long do you plan to hide out down here?" she challenged, her brows rising when Quay appeared shocked. "I can practically see your mood changing before my eyes even when I just vaguely mention Seattle. I want to know what's wrong with you."

The muscle in Quay's jaw danced wickedly as the rest of his features tightened. "You should know," he grumbled while splashing out of the pool.

Ty wasted no time following him back into the suite. "Would you mind clarifying that?"

"If we go back, I'm liable to break some necks, Ty. That clear enough for you?"

"Oh," she replied, barely able to swallow past the sudden lump in her throat. "Houston's neck, I take it?"

"And that bastard, Marcus."

Ty slipped into a white cotton robe and watched Quay pour himself a stiff drink from the bar. "Is it that bad?" she asked.

"It's that bad," Quay muttered, "when we aren't…together, torturing those jackasses is all I think about. Wait," he urged, when Ty opened her mouth to speak, "if you're about to tell me to let it go, I'm sorry. That ain't gonna happen unless I stay as far away from Seattle as possible."

Ty shook off the coldness that was brushing her skin and put on a teasing smile while heading toward the bar. "The last thing I want to do is share you with anyone," she murmured against his ear and linked her arms around his waist. She took away his glass when he turned in her arms, before pressing soft, wet pecks to his chest and jaw. "Now, where were we?" she asked.

Seattle, Washington

Josephine Ramsey opened the door to her bathroom suite just an inch and assessed the bedroom to see if it was empty. Pushing open the door a bit wider, she took a better look and saw that

Marcus had gone. Sighing her relief and delight, she left the bath. Lovely as it was, she was sick of spending the better part of an hour there waiting for her husband to leave for the day.

If only I had strength enough to leave him, she thought. All she had to do was pack and go. There were no small boys running around to wrangle and prepare for a trip to an unknown destination. She answered to no one but herself.

However, Josephine knew that for all her hatred and disgust for her husband, she'd not leave. Not now, not ever. Even though her sons had pretty much begged her to leave their own father in the dust, she knew she wouldn't. Did she love him that much? No, but she loved her life, her home. In short, she loved being Mrs. Marcus Ramsey. Sure she could have such a lifestyle away from him. Sadly, she'd grown accustomed to the label and the respect it garnered. She honestly didn't know who Josephine Simon was anymore. She didn't know how to live without the label. She didn't know how to live without being attached to a man.

Clearly it didn't matter what sort of man he was. The realizations about Houston and that he'd confided to Marcus about killing Sera…Marc not only kept those horrors a secret, but went so far as to arrange the disappearance of evidence and possibly assist in his brother's escape when he knew…

Josephine shook her head, not wanting to think about the rest. Houston had done more than have an affair with his daughter's best friend. He'd murdered her and that was only half the story.

Again, Josephine shook her head, sending locks of her bobbed cut into her face. She would go mad—well, more mad than she was already, if she didn't stop replaying this in her mind. For years, it had rested on her heart—lying dormant amidst a wealth of other horrors. Then, the case resurfaced, Houston's deeds were reborn and it was only a matter of time before the rest of the tale was revealed.

"This was totally unnecessary, you know? I could've easily gotten myself home," County told Fernando as they entered her exquisite condo in Library Tower.

"I don't know what possessed you to leave your truck at home and take the train in the first place," Fernando grumbled, unbuttoning the black leather trench he wore.

County tossed her coat to a nearby armchair. "First of all I, unlike you, am not chauffeured to work on the regular. Second, fighting rush hour traffic in Chicago ain't my idea of fun." She brushed nonexistent lint from her skirt. "Besides, winter just came too fast this year."

"Yeah January…what was old man winter thinking?" Fernando teased, earning a sour look from County in return.

"Careful Ramsey," she warned.

Her use of his last name again caused Fernando's gaze to narrow. He'd never cared for it, but hearing her say it... Damn, could this woman do anything to disinterest him?"

"Well, thank you for the ride," County said, clearing her throat when she noticed the intensity of his stare.

He smiled and glanced briefly towards the carpet. "Are you asking me to leave?"

"Yes."

"Then do it and stop beating around the bush. That's not like you."

Contessa almost smiled. He was right, of course. But this man—this incredible giant of a man was causing her silk over steel demeanor to slowly, noticeably erode.

"Get out," she said, since he'd closed the distance between them.

"That's more like it," he said with a wolfish grin.

"Then do it," County whispered and turned away.

Instead, Fernando followed her into the living room admiring the asymmetrical cut of the tweed skirt she wore. "What time should I pick you up tomorrow?"

"Tomorrow?" County asked, her confusion evident.

"Damn, you've already forgotten my offer to show you my life's work," he said, pretending to be offended.

"Ah," she gestured with a quick wave and roll of her eyes. "Please don't bother with that. I believe you. I believed you all along," she told him, leaning against the arm of a chocolate suede sofa. "You look like a man who enjoys dabbling in lots of different interests."

Fernando eased his hands inside his trouser pockets. "Complimenting me again?" he inquired.

"Can't you tell?"

Fernando only smirked his uncertainty. "I still want you to see the magazines."

"We're just so busy at the house right now and it's very hard for me to get away."

"You're the boss."

"Precisely why I have to be there."

"Even the boss deserves time away from her desk."

"Dammit Ramsey, why is this so important to you?"

"Because I want to spend more time with you," he admitted simply.

"Why?" she challenged, leaning back to get a better look at him. "Do you think it'll lead to something?"

He moved closer. "I think we're past that."

"You're right. We are and we won't ever pass that again," she sweetly promised.

Pulling his hands from his pockets, Fernando braced them on either side of her. "You really believe you'll never sleep with me again?"

County felt her heart flutter and ordered her lashes not to do the same. "I really believe that," she said, scanning his eyes, the slope of his nose, wide mouth and the lightly bearded square jaw.

Fernando seemed to consider her words before standing straight. "I guess I can buy that. After all, we didn't get much sleep then, did we?"

County moved off the arm of the chair. Her cheeks burned as images of them together flashed before her eyes. The things he did to her, the things they did to each other. She thought about it every day. Pleasure swirled through her at the mere memory of the delight she'd experienced. "What we did was a mistake—careless and immature. You must think I'm some sort of—"

"Stop," he ordered then, his voice brooking no argument. "Don't do that. I won't let you do that."

County raked shaking fingers across her dark cropped hair and turned. "Good night Ramsey," she sang, preparing to head for the door.

He blocked her path, his size easily allowing him to do so.

Resist him, resist him, she sang, focusing on the breadth of his chest as she dared not look him in the eyes. Her lips parted when his hand settled to the curve of her hip. The massive expanse of his palm massaged her there before angling around the generous swell of her bottom. She moaned when one light tug brought her into his incredible frame. A tiny hiss of a curse rose from her tongue as a wealth of sensation flooded her senses.

For several torturous moments, Fernando cupped her derriere, squeezing and grinding her into the powerful stiffness below his waist. His lips brushed her brow, temple and the line of her cheek. Choosing to forget her resistance, Contessa sought his mouth with her own. His tongue thrust hot and masterfully and she welcomed the power of the act. Whimpering amidst the passionate lunges inside her mouth, County's fingers curved weakly into his unyielding chest. When his tongue stroked the roof of her mouth and a low growl rose in his throat, Contessa felt her legs weaken. Fernando held her high to prevent her from slipping to the floor. His kiss was deep and branding—possession personified.

County scarcely noticed that he'd carried her with him to the front door. Her fingers were buried in the beautiful silk of his curly dark brown hair and she relished the power lying untapped within his magnificent frame.

"No going to that office of yours tomorrow. I'll be here by nine a.m.," he said.

"Okay," she agreed, sounding every bit the obedient little girl while arching closer for just another taste of his kiss.

Fernando obliged, plying her with a few more sultry probes of his persuasive tongue. County's eagerness and helpless murmurs into his mouth were almost his undoing, but he managed to ease away and set her to her feet.

"Good night," he said, brushing a smudge of lipstick from her cheek before he walked out the door.

Chapter 3

"You look surprised, Ramsey," County said at ten minutes past nine when she opened her door to Fernando.

"I expected you to be gone," he admitted, admiring the black cotton that emphasized the alluring fullness of her bosom.

Contessa stepped aside, waving him before her. "Now why would I do something like that?"

Fernando shrugged, pulling off the hunter green bomber jacket he wore over a sweater of the same color. "I figured you might be afraid to spend time with me."

"Ah, because you think I'm afraid of how you

affect me?" County inquired, rubbing her hands across the long sleeves that hugged her wrists.

Fernando came to tower over her. "That's right," he confirmed.

And it was true, yet County managed to maintain her cool. "We should eat first. You haven't had breakfast yet, have you?"

Fernando followed as she hurried towards the living room. "Where would you like to go?"

"Here."

Surprised, Fernando couldn't help but smile when he noticed the table arranged near the fireplace. "How thoughtful of you to order in."

County cast a tired glance across her shoulder. "Funny," she sighed, "I cooked."

"You cooked for me?" he asked, crossing his arms over his chest.

"I cooked for *us*," she corrected, then fixed him with a curious look. "Did I catch you off guard or something?"

"You strike me as the type of woman who'd frown on anything domestic," he confessed, watching as she moved around making last minute adjustments to the table setting. Silently, he noted that she was always seductively impeccable— nails, hair, even her face, void of makeup that morning, was perfect. A natural beauty, he decided, loving the way the black jeans molded to her curvaceous bottom.

"Growing up the way I did makes it impossible for me to be anything other than domestic, no matter how hard I try to run away from it."

The insight into her background intrigued Fernando and he sat on the back of the sofa to watch her. "So you've tried to run away from it?" he asked.

County uncovered the turkey bacon and shrugged. "A time or two."

"And?"

"You can never run away from who you really are," she said in a refreshing tone as though it were something she'd discovered after much searching.

Fernando grinned and Contessa found that she was captivated by the sound of the chuckle that dwelled within his chest. She watched him leave the sofa and come towards her. His steps were slow, purposeful and unwavering, she realized. His walk was a clear example of who he was: patient, determined and unrelenting. He wanted her and no matter how she tried to dismiss it—he wanted something beyond the physical. Beautiful, but was she ready for that? Was she ready for that from this clearly charismatic, clearly dangerous man?

He stopped before her, one massive hand rising to cup her chin. "You say you can never run from who you really are?" he probed, his thumb smoothing across the lush curve of her lips.

"That's right," she said, a slow tremble rising within her.

"I'd have to disagree. It can definitely be done given enough time and emotional distance."

He believed that so desperately, County thought, taking note of the increased strength in his voice when he uttered the words. She hadn't the heart to tell him he was wrong. She knew he needed to believe that he could actually be rid of his heritage in spite of the fact that it was bred within him.

"Well," she sighed, squeezing his hand until it lowered from her face. "I hope you like what I have."

Again, Fernando's translucent browns raked her hourglass frame and he could only shake his head in admiration.

"You really can cook," Fernando complimented later when their breakfast was nearing completion.

"I'm glad you're pleased," County said with a smile brightening her oval face. He had no idea how deeply his words delighted her.

Fernando dropped his napkin to the table and had the look of a completely satisfied man. "I expected to see a box of microwave blueberry pancakes and a bag of frozen hash browns. Not a mixing bowl and flour where you'd made the pancakes from scratch or real Idaho potatoes you'd cut up for the browns."

County laughed at his surprise. "I assure you that I take advantage of the shortcuts quite often."

"But what impresses me is you don't need to."

Okay, his flattery and admiration were really

pleasing her. Still, she didn't want to read any more into the moment. *Then why'd you cook for him, fool?* she berated herself before dismissing her unease.

"I hardly ever cook except when I take a day off for myself," she explained.

Fernando's long brows rose. "So you won't be going in today?"

"I had no idea how long it'd take for you to *impress* me, so to be on the safe side..."

"Right, right..." he drawled, taking part in her teasing. "Well, since it'll probably take me a while, we should go on and head out."

County was already pushing her chair away from the table. "Sounds good," she decided, collecting plates and silverware to take to the kitchen.

Together, they cleared the table, putting dishes in the washer and returning other items to the fridge and cupboards. All the time they were in awe of how easy the silence was between them. In spite of the very huge thing that had happened between them a few weeks earlier and whatever was going on between them now, they were comfortable with one another. For two people who'd spent the better part of their lives putting on fronts and masks to show how cool and unfazed they were, what they both craved was to find someone to shed the mask for.

Mick brushed away a heavy curl that had fallen into her face as she stood before the long spotlight mirror in the bathroom. There, she performed her daily ritual of inspecting her body for the tiniest changes. There was no doubting her pregnancy now—even though everyone else had said she was carrying the baby well and really wasn't showing much. Even her doctor wanted her to eat and put on more pounds.

Still, Mick could see the changes. Her amber gaze was soft as it roamed her belly the way her hands did. *Will I do right by you, little baby? I pray you won't be disappointed.*

The bathroom's white oak door opened a tad wider and Quest stuck his head inside. "You all right?" he inquired, smiling as his gray eyes raked her dark body.

"Dammit Quest," Mick hissed the moment she heard her husband's voice. Reaching for a bath sheet, she covered herself quickly. "Do you always have to just barge in like that?!"

Curious, Quest stepped farther into the bathroom. "Since when do you wear a towel around me?" he asked, folding his arms across his chest while he leaned against the doorjamb. "Unless you're tryin' to tease me?" he asked in a hopeful tone.

"Ha! With *this* body?" she snapped and turned away. "Not exactly what you're used to seeing," she grumbled.

"Damn right," he breathed.

Mick's face reflected hurt when she whirled

around to face him. "Thanks," she hissed, trying to move past him.

Quest caught her easily and pulled her with him where he made her lean against the counter. "You're right, you've changed," he confirmed, smiling when her lashes fluttered and she looked away. He tugged on her arms until she looked at him again. "Your body's even more—"

"Fat."

"Phenomenal," he corrected, his left dimpled grin appearing when he saw surprise reflected on her face.

Mick's eyes narrowed. "Don't make jokes Quest. Not now."

"That was no joke," he swore, his expression sharp with honesty as he pressed his forehead to hers. "You're carrying my child inside your body. To me, that's more phenomenal than any size five frame bouncing around before me."

"Size four," she corrected, giggling when he tickled her.

"Four or forty-four, I love you," he vowed and pulled away the towel she still clutched. "Are you off limits yet?" he asked, grinning devilishly when she shook her head no. Rising to his full height, he pulled her high against him.

"That's the best thing I've heard today."

Mick kicked away the towel still tangled between them and arched into his kiss.

* * *

Fernando shook his head and marveled at the scene that had already replayed itself four times. He and Contessa arrived at Hood Don Publications which housed *Male Desire* and *Threads* magazines. They'd visited several departments and, in the male dominated environment, County held everyone's attention.

They were all impressed by her stature in the publishing industry, that was the excuse they used to stay close to her. Fernando knew the truth, she was a luscious beauty who practically wore her appeal like a negligee. He'd already given the guys more time visiting than he'd planned to. Therefore, he was unsympathetic to their disappointment when he announced that it was time for him and Contessa to head out. He massaged his eyes as the guys crowded around in greater number to say their goodbyes to County. A second or two passed before he was pulled aside by his chief editor, Perry Graves.

"Just when I thought you couldn't possibly top yourself, man. She's somethin' else," Perry commended.

"Yes, she is," Fernando agreed, smirking as he watched County revel in the attention she received. "She's also tough and complex," he confided.

Perry sent his friend a sympathetic glance. "Be careful. Those are the women you want to keep."

"I know," he agreed with a slow nod.

"Perry," County called, walking over to shake hands, "it was so nice to meet you. You've got an impressive place here."

"Thank you Contessa," Perry said, squeezing both her hands. "I hope to see you again," he said. "I have a feeling I will," he added for Fernando's ears only.

"I apologize for any doubts I had about your business," County said as she and Fernando made their way toward the elevators. "You seem to have a great company—great staff."

"Thanks, but I promise you it didn't all come together overnight," he cautioned.

"I can just imagine how impressive your Seattle business must be," she complimented while toying with the brown and black fringe trim of her mosaic print knit coat. She glanced up in time to see the stoniness take control of his gaze. Clearly his *other* operations were a subject off-limits. "So where are we off to next?" she asked, hoping to dispel some of the tension.

His grin returned. "I want to show you my club, but you might want to grab some lunch first."

"Well, can't we eat at the club?" she asked, as they stepped onto the elevator car. "Or isn't your club that advanced?" she teased, noticing the uncertainty flash on his face.

"The atmosphere might affect your appetite," he said, smoothing his big hands together as though he were trying to find the right way to phrase the statement.

County understood. "So it's a gentleman's club?" she asked, watching his long lashes close over his eyes in confirmation. "Ramsey, do you really think a few naked women would rile me?"

"I wouldn't feel right about having you eat lunch here," he said, more preoccupied by what she'd think than he realized.

County found his unease adorable. She almost prayed that he'd do something that wasn't charming or sensual. Her list of reasons to discourage a relationship with the man was already way too short.

Seattle, Washington

Anson Carter and Graham Johnson felt their hearts drop clear to their stomachs when Sheila McPhereson announced that the boss would see them. The two exchanged looks of sheer dread and followed the executive secretary down the corridor which seemed even longer in the wake of their pending meeting with one of the Dark Squires partners.

Sheila kept a few steps ahead of them giving Anson and Graham the chance to make last minute brush-ups to their explanations.

"Dammit, he shouldn't bite off our heads over this. After all, it was his partner who told us to back off," Graham reasoned.

"You really want to call the man out like that?" Anson queried.

Graham rolled his eyes. "Brotha, right now I'll do anything to ensure that my ass is still attached to my body when I walk out of here."

Anson smirked. "Amen," he agreed.

Sheila waved Anson and Graham toward the slightly ajar double doors. She was about to see them inside when she was instructed by the office's occupant to do otherwise. "Good luck guys," she whispered before walking off.

Anson and Graham inhaled and then stepped into the lion's den—literally.

Stefan Lyons was one half of the team that operated Dark Squires Communications. The privately owned company had remained so because the two partners had no desire for a board or stockholders overseeing and dictating their every move. That was especially true since the moves were often risky, usually ruthless and frequently dangerous.

Seated behind his desk, Stefan puffed on a long cigar. It was his favorite pastime and a habit that made him seem far older than he was. He waved for the two men to have a seat and enjoyed several more puffs of his cigar.

"Do you two have the contract for Contessa House?" he asked them.

Graham leaned forward. "Stef, we tried, but we—"

"Do you two have the contract for Contessa House?" Stef voiced the question once again.

Anson folded one hand over Graham's arm. "No," he answered.

"Let me explain why I send two men on sales trips," Stef said after enjoying a few more puffs from his cigar. "Two men ensure that the pitch will be thoroughly understood by the client. A second man points out valuable facts to the client—facts that his partner may've failed to mention—thus providing the client with a deal they can't refuse. But you *two* failed. Now what do you think I should do about that?"

Anson and Graham exchanged glances and knew it was time to pull out all the stops lest they be fired…or worse.

"Can we at least explain?" Graham raised his hand to ask.

"You didn't close the deal. That's all I need to know."

"No, it's not, Stef."

The room went deathly still. Graham closed his eyes, knowing a few of his friend's teeth were about to be strewn across the Oriental rug that covered half the floor.

Instead, Stef seemed interested and came to sit on the edge of his spotless pine desk. "What do you think I need to know?"

"We didn't have a chance to complete the pitch because we were told to leave," Anson shared quickly.

Stef rolled his eyes. "That's what the client

usually does when they deal with piss poor salesmen."

"No Stef, it was Fernando," Graham said.

"Fernando?" Stef repeated, curious and mildly
stunned. "I'm surprised he even decided to attend the
meeting.

"He didn't attend the meeting," Anson clarified.

"He was there meeting with two centerfolds for
one of his Chicago magazines," Graham added.

Stef took a long drag from his cigar. "So my
partner just happened to be there, huh?"

"He arranged it," Graham confessed.

Stef nodded. "Go on," he urged, leaving the
corner of his desk.

"We'd been talking to Ms. Warren for a while, when
he gave a nod signaling that we should leave," Graham
continued, "we didn't think it'd be wise to argue."

"You thought right," Stef agreed, losing some of
his anger. "You guys go on home, relax, take a good
shower and the rest of the week off," he instructed.

Very relieved, Anson and Graham thanked their
boss and hurried toward the door.

"Guys?" Stef called, before their hands touched
the knob. "Tell me about Contessa Warren."

Anson's and Graham's smiles were the epitomes
of male satisfaction.

"You should see her Stef, a real dime," Anson ap-
praised.

Graham nodded. "Incredible body and an even

more incredible face. Plus, she's smart. Quick, outspoken, She's no fool."

"Yeah, if I weren't sitting across from her, I'd have sworn I was dealing with a man," Anson shared.

While his men flàttered Contessa, Stef nodded. *He's sleeping with her, or planning to,* he realized. "Thanks guys, get home and get some rest."

"Are you gonna forget the House, boss?" Graham wanted to know.

"No, just taking a different route," Stef confided.

Alone in the office, Stef finished off his cigar. Reaching for the private phone directory on his desk, he browsed the gold-trimmed pages until he found what he was looking for. He dialed the number and waited for the connection.

"Hey, it's Stef. I got a job for you. In Chicago. Contessa Warren. I want to know everything about her."

Chapter 4

The Spot was an upscale gentleman's club located several miles outside of Chicago. To an average passerby, the place looked like an elaborate mansion. A tour inside the dwelling, however, showed it was far more than that.

County was in awe. She had never seen the inside of such a club, in spite of what many of her friends believed. Fernando strolled through the house noting several points of interest. County was especially surprised to find women dancing in both dark and well-lit rooms.

"I believe in giving my patrons a choice," Fernando said as they strolled the mammoth-sized establishment. "I found that many prefer the well-lit rooms to the dark ones."

"It's such a huge place," County cited, her eyes wider as they scanned the high ceilings and tall windows lining the corridors and upper levels. "There's dancing in all these rooms, huh?" she inquired softly.

Fernando chuckled at her candor and was about to provide her with an explanation when they were interrupted. County tried not to stare at the man who was as massive as Fernando, but looked as though his life had been much rougher—much deadlier.

Fernando nodded, and then drew the man over to where she stood. "Contessa Warren, this is Mbeki Carpenter, one of my partners here in the club."

County smiled and extended her hand. "Pleasure to meet you," she greeted, clearing her throat when the man's hand practically smothered her own.

"Very nice to meet you," Mbeki replied, his light brown eyes trailing her face appreciatively. "This won't take long, Fern," he said, before leaving County with another smile and nod.

"Will you be all right on your own for a few minutes?" Fernando asked her, his concern evident.

County waved her hand. "I'll be fine. Go handle your business," she urged, already turning to study a few of the portraits that lined the walls. Of course, she was covertly studying the two giants down the hall.

Clearly something was wrong. When Mbeki uttered only a few words, Fernando's expression turned murderous. The two spoke for several minutes more, and then shook hands and parted ways. County figured their date was over, but she was mistaken.

"Are you really sure about eating here County?" he asked, a furrow settling between his brows.

"I'm positive. Unless…there's a problem? Your conversation seemed pretty serious."

Fernando shook his head and stroked his hair roughened jaw. "Just a few personnel issues," he explained.

"Would you like to discuss them?"

"No, I would not," Fernando replied promptly, grinning at the cool, airy manner she posed the question.

"Well, you never did answer my other question anyway," she pointed out.

"And that was?" Fernando queried, folding his arms across his chest.

"About all the rooms in the house."

"What about them?"

County's mouth fell open. "You're kidding? You really don't know what I'm asking?"

"Just what do you *think* goes on in all these rooms?" he asked in a quiet voice.

County smoothed her hands across the wool knit fabric of her coat. "I'm sure *you* know very well what goes on in them."

He took a step closer to her. "As far as I know eating and dancing."

"There're many ways to dance, Ramsey."

"Don't I know it."

"So?"

"So as far as I know everything that goes on here is strictly professional and legal."

"As far as you know," County rephrased, her wide brown eyes suspicion filled. "Is that your way of saying that you don't know how the ladies make… extra money?"

Fernando's expression went deadly serious. "That's my way of saying I make infrequent unannounced visits to the club at least three times a month. In all those times, I've never witnessed anything happening under the table or between the sheets. Do you understand what I'm saying?"

County only pressed her lips together and nodded.

"Good," he said, taking her upper arms in a light grasp. "Now can we please eat?"

County's gasp seemed to echo when she and Fernando entered one of the upstairs rooms. It was an exquisite area illuminated by soft lighting and warmed by a gorgeous fireplace. Relaxing classical jazz swirled throughout.

"Is this just for us?" County breathed, her brown leather boots disappearing into a rich burgundy carpet.

"All the rooms look this way." Fernando seemed to take great pride in sharing with her. "My guests come to dine here."

"So they have dinner along with their private dances," County noted, casting Fernando a suggestive look as he held her chair.

"There's no *private* dances," he informed her after taking his place at the table. "Only dances for private *parties* of ten or more plus security to ensure my rules are followed."

"So strict," Contessa drawled, leaning back in the chair she occupied. "It's a wonder you're able to keep girls, or clients for that matter."

Fernando toyed with the silverware on the table. "Rules ensure I have the most beautiful and intelligent girls and gentlemanly and intelligent clients," he schooled her.

County propped her chin to her fist. "Some might find that boring."

"Precisely why I wouldn't have to worry about them working for me or becoming clients," Fernando said, his translucent brown gaze firm and steady. "These men come to unwind after a vicious corporate day. They want to conduct *boring* business and find that having a beautiful woman in the vicinity makes the task far more enjoyable."

County tilted her water glass in a mock toast. "Smart," she commended.

"Thank you."

"Profitable?"

"Very."

A side door opened in the private dining room and a very handsome young man walked in. He greeted Fernando in his heavy Spanish brogue and then kissed Contessa's hand before asking if they'd like to order drinks.

"Whiskey sour," County ordered, returning his dazzling smile with one of her own.

"Scotch neat. Thanks Manny," Fernando said.

"Is he part of your dance troupe?" County asked when they were alone.

"One of my chefs," Fernando informed while reaching for a menu, "I thought you'd approve."

"Oh, I do," she replied softly, perusing her own menu. "So why do you do it?" she asked, after they'd been studying the dining selections for quite a while.

"What?" Fernando asked.

"Run your club this way? It's out in the middle of nowhere," she reasoned when he fixed her with a curious look. "Clearly your clients are men of power. No one would ask questions. No one would know."

"I'd know," he immediately returned. "It's taken me a long time to go legit, County. It's difficult when you go it alone."

"Your friends didn't approve?" she asked, keeping her eyes focused on the menu.

"I lost a lot of friends when I told them I didn't want that life."

"Admirable. That you'd cut them all off."

He grinned. "I didn't cut them all off, but they know and have accepted that they'll have to go straight if they expect to have my assistance."

County brought her wide brown stare to his face. "And you're sure they've gone straight?"

"As far as I know," he said, chuckling when she burst into laughter.

"This whining of yours has gone way past pissin' me off, Houston," Marcus growled, rubbing his bloodshot eyes as he paced behind the bar in his office. He groaned, cursing himself when his words set off another pitiful rant from his younger brother. "Houston!" he roared finally, ordering himself to calm when he obtained silence. "This has got to stop Hous. It's wearin' the hell out of me and I'm sick of it. All this damn complaining…you know how many men would kill to be where you are?"

"Hmph. So that's how I got here."

"Get over it Houston and just count your lucky stars that you're not sittin' up in some jail."

"Don't you try that crap on me Marc," Houston snapped, his voice taking on a strength all of a sudden. "You got just as much to lose here as I do. Maybe more."

"Weak bastard. Don't you dare threaten me," Marc ordered, not about to let the man know how true his words were. "Hell, you can have and do anything your heart desires."

"Anything?" Houston pouted. "Anything like see my wife?"

"Please," Marc spat, slamming a beaded glass to the bar. "Since when? Since when do you care about spending time with your wife? Certainly not while you were out screwing all your daughter's friends."

"Damn you."

"Damn *me?*" Marc retorted with a chuckle. "I don't think you want that, my man. After all, I'm your only damn friend. I think even Daphne would turn your ass over to the cops if she knew where you were."

Houston knew it was true, his hand clenching and unclenching as he stared over the beautiful Hawaiian sky without really seeing it. He thought of all the months he'd been on the run with no word to his family. He wondered if they even missed him with the shame he'd cast their way. "Just get me out of here, Marc," he begged quietly. "I'm sick every day and—"

"Please with the complaining, dammit," Marc interrupted, sloshing more bourbon into his glass. "I'll work everything out and I'll be in touch, all right?" he said and slammed down the phone just as Houston began to speak again.

The crystal goblet hit with a loud shatter. Josephine watched glass and liquid stream the wall of her reading room. After lounging in bed until midmorning, she came to lounge down there until late afternoon. It was her daily ritual and it was pathetic. Today, a trip down memory lane was the cause of the glass of vodka being smashed against the wall.

Josephine pushed her hair from her face and looked through eyes blurred by tears at the pages of her wedding album. Even on that day, the bride in those pictures had eyes filled with uncertainty, shame and fear.

Marcus Ramsey had literally swept her off her feet. She was the youngest in a family of five girls. Of course, her older sisters believed they'd be the ones to catch the eye of the gorgeous second son of Quentin and Marcella Ramsey. When Josephine caught his eye, they were stunned and she was giddy with delight over their displeasure.

It was like a dream and Marc spared no expense where she was concerned. He knew that she was innocent to the ways of men. Josephine couldn't help but smile in memory of the gentle and attentive manner he treated her in the early days. Unfortunately, she learned too late that he wanted her innocent—dumb to a man's true motives. She was a trophy, an arm piece to give him a pristine public appearance that would shield his true nature.

He hadn't even the decency to wait until after they were married to show his true colors. Josephine slammed her palm to the photo of the bride and groom, cursing herself for not having sense enough to run as fast as she could. She had a ton of pride, though, and quickly learned the meaning of the bible verse "God hates pride." Pride made a person do, say and behave in the most heinous fashion. Josephine realized that she simply didn't want her jealous sisters to know that her prince charming was a toad of the most evil sort.

"You didn't enjoy your meal?" Fernando asked, setting aside his napkin as he studied the expression on County's face. He tilted his head inquisitively when she finally smiled.

"The meal was great," she assured him in a soft voice.

"Then what's wrong?"

County clenched her hands atop the intimate round table and regarded him with uneasy eyes. "I just wanted to apologize."

Fernando was stumped. "Apologize?"

"I gave you such a hard time when you told me there was nothing shady going on here at the club," she clarified. "I know you were offended and I'm sorry."

"Don't worry about it," he said with a wave of one hand.

County shook her head. "I have to. Especially since I know what it's like to have people think the worst of you."

"You know what that's like?" Fernando asked, a

soft chuckle mingling with the words. "I have a hard time believing that, since everyone you meet seems to love you."

Contessa grinned. "That's part of the problem," she said, taking a sip of her refreshed drink. "Men love me because they're taken by my demeanor— seductive, boisterous, challenging—*easy*," she said with a roll of her eyes. "Then they find out that last one isn't so accurate and the seductive element turns to a tease, boisterous and challenging are labeled as bitchy. And we won't go into what the women think."

In spite of her light, unaffected manner, Fernando knew she hurt deeply from such treatment. He knew that her seductive, boisterous and challenging qualities were masks she used to hide the hurt.

"Well, I'm stuffed," she said, patting her non-existent tummy.

Fernando stood. "Then let's get the hell out of here."

"I'm leaving tomorrow."

County blinked, but kept her gaze focused past the car window when she heard him. Knowing he hadn't shared the tidbit just to pass time, she swallowed the lump of emotion lodged in her throat and turned. "Have a good trip," she told him.

"Come with me," he said.

Mouth open, County watched Fernando for

countless moments. She was waiting for him to smile and nudge her shoulder as if to say "Just playin'"—she received no such indication.

"You're joking?" she presumed.

"I'm not."

"That's crazy."

"Why?"

"So many, *too* many reasons," she went on, barely able to hear anything over her heartbeat. "Where would we go?"

"I have business in Seattle."

"Ha! Reason number one. Aside from all the reasons you *must* be aware of, I'll label the obvious. I'm your father's least favorite person. It'd be hell for you."

Fernando's handsome caramel-toned face registered pure disgust. "I don't give a damn about my father. If anything I want you more because of his disapproval."

"Thanks," County whispered, raking him with a scathing look.

He turned on the seat. "You know what I mean. I have business in Seattle, but it can wait. We can go anywhere," he promised her.

County couldn't look away from the penetrating tug of his light stare. She was almost thoroughly intoxicated by him and in desperate need of a lifeline.

"I barely know you," she tried.

"So come and get to know me then," he challenged.

County shook her head. "This is crazy and we both have businesses to run. Besides, this won't wind up with us in bed again so—"

The kiss to cut off her words rendered her weak and willing at once. Soft moans filled the dark interior of the car. County pressed her hands to Fernando's chest with every intention of pushing him away. The brick wall she encountered only forced a breathless cry past her lips. She could almost feel the rumble of an impassioned growl deep inside him as he lay sprawled across her. His tongue thrust lustily and hot. His hands tightened on her waist when she suckled his lower lip and became an eager participant in the wet, possessive kiss.

Fernando was almost out of his mind with wanting her. He'd thought of kissing her all day and could no longer restrain himself. Her helpless cries in his ear filled him with a cocky certainty to know he affected her so. Her curvaceous form filled his hands, beckoning him to fondle and squeeze until his heart was content. He feared, however, that his heart wouldn't be content for quite some time. He felt desperate to have her near and knew he'd take whatever part of herself she was willing to give.

Contessa felt the raw emotion behind the kiss. It was an emotion that went far beyond desire, something deeper than anything physical. She'd never lost her composure with a man. Never—in any situation. She was always in control—always the winner of the game. But this man…

"Come with me," Fernando urged again, only breaking the kiss to voice the command against her ear.

County buried her fingers in the rich silk of his deep brown curls. "I can't," she moaned.

Fernando spent but a few moments longer kissing her jaw, the line of her neck and dip of her collarbone. "If you think I only want you in my bed," he murmured against her skin and was drugged by her perfume, "I'll admit it. I do. I want you there very much. I want more too and it scares the hell out of me." His deep-set gaze was intense and haunting.

"But you don't even know me," County pointed out, barely able to speak as she struggled to catch her breath.

He grinned. "I think that's why I'm scared. I won't stop seeing you Contessa. Please don't ask me to," he spoke in the same breath.

County tugged her bottom lip between her teeth and raked his hair roughened jaw with her nails.

"I won't lie and say that thinking of making love to you doesn't occupy a great deal of my thoughts," he shared as though he knew she still harbored reservations about his motives. "Just please don't think making love is *all* I want from you."

County couldn't move—couldn't look away from his engrossing stare until he glanced up. It was then she noticed they'd returned to her building. She prayed not to stumble or worse, fall, as the driver escorted her to the door.

Chapter 5

Fernando was true to his word. He visited Contessa faithfully for the next few weeks. Often, he arrived at her office by the end of work on Friday. Every woman who worked for Contessa House made a point of finding last-minute tasks to complete in order to catch a glimpse and perhaps a friendly smile or greeting from their boss's gorgeous, incredibly built gentleman caller.

County was no less immune. She felt as though she were caught up in a dream. Although Fernando's visits were brief, they whetted her appetite for more.

She even found herself dreading that she'd have to toil through eight hours of work on Friday before seeing him.

"County? County? You with us, hon?"

Blinking, County fixed Spivey and Jenean with absent looks, before tuning in finally to where she was: her office for the weekly meeting on the Ramsey book. Clearing her throat, she ordered her head out of the clouds or, more accurately, away from Fernando Ramsey.

"I'm with you," she assured them.

"So it looks like Marcus Ramsey is by far one of the family's most colorful characters," Spivey went on.

Jenean waved toward County. "Well, you've met him, girl. Are we on track? Spending more hours researching him? You think it's worth it?"

"Well, what have we got so far?" County asked, toying with one of the buttons on the formfitting blazer of her champagne metallic tweed skirt.

"Aside from assisting in his brother's disappearance and the disappearance of evidence—"

"Or so it's suspected," Spivey interrupted.

Jenean nodded. "Anyway, we're looking for any inconsistencies within his business dealings."

County nodded and put on a good show of being interested in the rundown on the Ramsey elder. Alas, her thoughts had turned once again to his son. Today was Friday. Fernando was coming and she felt as anxious as a kid waiting for the school's out bell to ring.

"County?"

Again, Contessa shook her head and commanded herself to focus. "I'm sorry," she whispered.

Jenean exchanged a knowing look with Spivey and then fixed her boss with a sympathetic smile. "We know you're seeing his son, County. If you'd prefer we not—"

"No, no, no, don't do that Jenean."

"But County we can understand if—"

"No Spivey," County ordered, her lovely wide gaze sparkling with determination. "This is our business and we've been working on this damn book too long to just chuck it." She told them, nodding when the concerned expressions Spivey and Jenean wore faded to satisfaction.

Silently, she chastised herself. She was becoming some sappy, daydreaming woman, letting herself be wooed by the king of Casanovas. But, damn it all, she didn't care, not when what he offered was so sweet and innocent.

Innocent? Contessa almost chuckled, having linked the word to what she shared with Fernando. The description however, was, for the most part, true. Their time together was simple and easy—dinner, a show, a jazz concert, a movie…or they stayed in. Aside from taking her hand to help her from the car or keeping his palm at the small of her back as they walked, he hadn't touched her. County believed such gentlemanly behavior was more torturous than a full-blown kiss.

I could never lose my heart to a man like Fernando Ramsey, she told herself, only to have a louder voice tell her, *foolish girl, you already have.*

"Do you think this is fair to her, man? She's finally happy to be in Seattle and you're keeping her away."

Quay closed his eyes and clutched the receiver in a tighter grip. He'd phoned Quest to discuss business and the conversation quickly turned to when he was coming home.

"Look Q, I'll tell you what I told Ty. When she talks about Seattle, I think about breakin' someone's neck."

Quest massaged his eyes while reclining in the chair behind his desk. "I hate 'em too Quay, but no way in hell am I gonna let them have power enough to keep me from home."

"I'll kill 'em if I see 'em Q."

"You're entitled to feel that way," Quest told his brother, grinning as an idea came to mind. "Tell you what, if you see Marc or Houston, you can have at 'em for five minutes before I pull you off."

"I need more time!" Quay laughed.

"All right, fifteen minutes!" Quest promptly extended.

Quay rapped his knuckles on the message table he relaxed behind. "Done," he said.

"Seriously?" Quest probed.

"Q man, I know it's time and I know I've been hiding out down here. It's just so easy, you know? It's so good being all alone—alone with the only person who completes me."

"I know exactly what you mean," Quest said, smiling as visions of his own wife filled his mind.

"How is she?" Quay asked, knowing where his brother's thoughts were centered.

"Crying because she's getting fat," Quest shared with a low chuckle, "and drivin' me out of my mind because I want her more now than I ever did."

Quay grinned, folding one arm across his chest and enjoying listening to his brother. Clearly Quest was even more in love with Michaela now than ever. The strength of such love only made him more content and grateful for the love he'd been blessed to find.

"So, she's finally settling in to the idea of becoming a mama?" Quay asked, when Quest silenced.

"I think she's got a ways to go, but I'd rather have her stressing over stretch marks than trying to hunt down leads to a killer."

Quay nodded, understanding his brother's relief. "That's why I didn't say anything."

"About?" Quest probed, crossing his sneaker shod feet atop his desk.

"Well, I didn't want Mick getting all caught up in the Sera Black case again and I didn't want it creeping into my time with Tyke, but I can't get the case out of my head."

"So spill it."

"I keep thinking about what Wake said when I saw him on the train to Banff."

Quest massaged the brand on his arm. "What about it?" he asked.

"When he started talking, he reminded me of how we met. During the interview his mom had to be our uncle's assistant."

"Marc," Quest supplied.

"Mmm…what keeps bothering me is that Wake said he'd been working for the man who was responsible for this."

"Houston," Quest said.

"It'd seem he's the one the evidence points to, but what if he'd been working for Marc?"

Quest's sleek brows drew close. "Quay, what the hell are you sayin'?"

"It'd make more sense. His mom was already working for him."

"Do you think Marc killed Sera?"

"No, no nothin' like that," Quay denied, massaging the back of his neck as he stood, "but I know the man has skeletons in his closet and if he used Wake to clean up Houston's mess, maybe he used him for other things too."

Quest's left dimple flashed as he pressed his lips together and considered his brother's theory. "Things… things that could affect the family," he noted.

"Mmm hmm and not for the good," Quay predicted.

* * *

"Could we be overreacting about this, y'all?" Fernando asked his managers at The Spot where they met to discuss the sudden loss of personnel. "I mean, it's not unusual for a woman to want out of this line of work no matter how nice *we* think the arrangement might be," he pointed out.

"It's just strange to lose so many girls in such a short span of time," Mbeki Carpenter said.

"Maybe someone latched onto a better position." Fernando debated, shrugging lazily. "Maybe she wanted to share the wealth."

"A better position?" Terence Newsome inquired. "Fern, you think we're bein' taken by another club?"

"Do we know of any new clubs in the area?" he asked, after silence filled the room for almost a minute. "Ones that would boast the same benefits as The Spot?" He stared out over the huge back lawn from his office window at the east wing of the mansion.

Silence again. Clearly, no one had an answer. At least, not an answer they were comfortable admitting.

"I suggest then, that we start sniffin' around some of the clubs. The ones we *do* know about," Fernando instructed, turning to fix his four managers with stern looks. "Let's see if they're havin' the same problem. Then try talking with a few of the girls and see if they know anything."

"Already covered Fern."

Everyone turned to see The Spot's only assistant manager Barry Evans walking past the office's double mahogany doors.

"Sorry I'm late Fern," Barry apologized.

Fernando waved his hand. "What'd you find?"

"I spoke with two of the girls we lost. They got jobs with Hoover Lyles."

"The travel agent?" Mbeki blurted.

"Mmm," Barry confirmed with a nod and then smiled as the room came alive with male laughter.

Fernando even chuckled at the news. Hoover Lyles was a former customer who was quite success- ful until his overpriced travel agency was labeled a sham. The extravagant prices bought vacations which were far from extravagant.

"What's he got 'em doing?" Fernando asked, leaning against the edge of his desk and waiting for Barry's response.

"Well, the girls told me they weren't even sure at first," he shared, skepticism creeping into his dark brown eyes. "They were told not to say a word about the offer because it was so secretive. They were finally approved after forwarding a portfolio and résumé."

"Portfolio and résumé?" Chase Shefford, another manager, asked.

Mbeki grunted. "Sounds shady," he said.

"What are they doing?" Fernando asked.

"That's the strange part," Barry said and leaned

forward to brace his elbows on his knees. "The job hasn't even started yet and they're already getting paid. Tell you the truth Fern, I don't even think the girls know what they're doing."

This began another round of discussion amongst the managers. While their voices were raised in debate, Fernando caught Barry's eye and waved him close.

"Do what you have to and find out exactly what type of position this is," he ordered.

Contessa didn't realize she'd been crying until she'd closed the door to her condo, removed her gloves and touched her face. Obviously, she'd been trying to remain cool in front of her employees. She'd looked disappointed enough when Fernando didn't show for his weekly visit. When someone mentioned that it was Valentine's Day and they were all excited to see what he'd do for her, she felt her heart drop. Clearly, he wasn't ready to spend time with her on such an *emotional* holiday. County told herself she was fine with that. After all, she wasn't ready either, right?

"Get it together," she ordered herself shortly and hefted one of the huge Ramsey files she asked Spivey to give over before she left the office. She'd have plenty of time to go through it this weekend she noted grimly and dropped the file to the credenza.

Unbuttoning the fur-trimmed leather trench, she

was about to remove it when something stopped her. There was an infrequent flashing originating someplace deep within the condo. It moved in a frantic fashion and flickered in the most mesmerizing way. The effect beckoned her closer instead of commanding her to turn and race out of the house.

In the living room, she found a beautifully set table for two before a roaring blaze in the fireplace. Roses had been sprinkled upon the floor where the table sat. The room smelled lightly of the scent. Her curiosity mounting, she stepped closer, observing the romantic scene. Soft music drifted about, something lovely and unrecognizable. Oriental perhaps? Whatever the genre, it only intensified the allure of the environment.

"I'm sorry I missed you at the office."

His voice resounded below the music. Contessa turned to find him leaning against the living room's entryway.

"I had a meeting that ran late," Fernando explained, easing his hands into the pockets of the gray nylon sweats he wore, "I wanted to get this done before you got home."

"What is this?" County breathed, her hand raised to wave weakly toward the room.

Fernando chuckled and smoothed his knuckles across his beard. "You so hard you don't think about Valentine's Day?" he mused.

County's lashes fluttered as she turned to observe

the table again. Swooning was a definite possibility as she was thoroughly affected by the seduction surging in the air. She jumped, feeling Fernando behind her as he moved to help her out of her coat. She prayed for her breathing to slow, as the action only caused her breasts to nudge his hands when they curved around the lapels of the trench. Of course, Fernando made a point of touching every part of her body he could reach. His fingers stroked the underside of one breast while his thumb softly manipulated a firming nipple. The caresses were so deliciously subtle, she could feel every part of her weakening in response.

"Are you hungry?"

County opened her mouth to say yes, but no words were forthcoming. She heard him utter another chuckle and knew he was both aware and pleased by her reaction to his closeness.

"Go change," he instructed, having removed the coat and unfastened the oversized buttons on her short-waist tweed blazer. "It'll be time to eat when you come back," he promised.

Like an obedient child, County nodded and headed out of the living room. Sadly, once she approached her bedroom door, her feet refused to move one step farther. Her mind was racing. No...actually, it was more like she was in a hazy state of mind. Her entire body shook and she could barely press a hand to her forehead, it trembled so. There had never been a man who made her feel so out of control, so wondrously light-headed. He'd accomplished this by doing the most minute things. She couldn't get her bearings and felt as if she were being led by some invisible thread.

Is this what it feels like to be swept off your feet? She wondered. *Is this what it feels like to fall in love?* She cleared her throat at the thought and forced herself into the bedroom.

There, she received another shock. The room had undergone a serious transformation. The place was alive with candlelight. Her bed teemed with rose petals and the exotic melody she'd heard out front was playing steadily.

Slowly, County reached for one of the petals and pressed it against her nose. The beautiful cream and coral drapes had been drawn to reveal the view of snowfall past the windows. She was both relaxed and energized by the cozy aura and the sensuality coursing through her. Then, she knew she wasn't alone and turned to find Fernando leaning against the doorjamb.

"How?" was all she could ask.

He needed no further clarification. "You've got the sweetest landlady. She remembered me from the times I've visited before. When I told her what I wanted to do, she let me and my team come in and work our magic," he explained as though it were no big deal.

"Why?" she inquired, feeling like a dope only capable of producing one-word questions.

Fernando had shortened the distance between them. "I've told you why," he said, cupping her small oval face in his hands. "Now let me show you."

County pressed both hands to the concrete wall of his chest and resisted what she wanted most. "Is this because you want to have sex with me?" she whispered, watching his eyes crinkle when he began to smile.

Fernando moved his hands to her hips. "No, it's because I want to make love with you."

Contessa knew she had never once in her life moaned because of something a man said. That night, she did. Any thought of resistance or reason why this was right or wrong fled her mind. She eagerly surrendered to the massive caramel god who held her so gently in his powerful embrace.

Fernando trailed his mouth from her temple to the curve of her cheek before deciding her earlobe was his preferred spot. Contessa felt herself trembling all over again as he eased her down to sit on the bed. Kneeling before her, he removed the mocha stilettos and briefly applied massaging pressure to her heels. Strong fingers began a possessive ascent up her calves and thighs to find the waistband of her sheer stockings. He paused at the junction of her thighs, and County's lashes fluttered closed when his thumbs assaulted the extra sensitive flesh that guarded the entrance to her womanhood.

A second or three passed and the nylons and panties were gone. Fernando drove his thumb deep inside, his gorgeous browns narrowing when she cried out her appreciation. County relaxed a bit on her bed, allowing him more room to explore. She moved to undo the fastening of her skirt, but he stopped her by closing his hand over hers. His thumb still plunged madly inside her while he took her mouth in a feverish kiss. County made deep breathless sounds as her tongue dueled with his.

"Get me out of this thing," she begged, desperately wanting the skirt off her body.

Fernando chuckled. "In time," he promised, deciding to relieve her of the formfitting blazer first.

County curved her hands around his neck, her fingers rubbing through the luxurious softness of his hair. She wriggled out of the blazer when he pulled it from her shoulders, along with the black camisole beneath. His hands cupped beneath her arms to settle her to the middle of the satin covered queen-sized bed. He would not remove her bra, and instead nibbled at the flawless honey-toned skin that bubbled over the tops of the lacy garment. Contessa arched her back and begged him to see to the nipples straining for attention. She felt an overwhelming amount of moisture against her thighs and knew she was seconds away from becoming orgasmic.

"Please Ramsey, please…"

"Patience."

"I can't," she cried softly, tugging on the edge of the black T-shirt he still wore.

Fernando took her wrists and held them above her head. She had the power to satisfy him too soon if he lost control. He'd waited long enough to have her to let the moment pass in a blur.

County flexed her fingers against the covers where her hands were trapped. After a while Fernando removed her bra and then scooped a handful of the rose petals that still littered the bed and sprinkled them across her bare skin. County shivered, feeling the tufts of silk next to her breasts. Fernando cupped the mounds and buried his face between them, inhaling the floral fragrance and the intoxicating scent of her perfume.

Contessa's hands were freed, but she couldn't move them. She lay there, moving upon the bed as though she were in the midst of fever. The satiny flowers mingling with the roughness of his beard was an indescribable feeling. Her soft gasps waltzed with Fernando's tortured groans as he suckled and nibbled mercilessly. He finally relieved her of the skirt and took a moment to appraise her form. The low lighting cast more gold to her honey complexion. His fingers trailed every dip and curve as if he were in awe.

"Please," she urged, tugging on his shirt and pressing her lips together when his eyes met hers.

Fernando granted the request, allowing her fingers to splay across the chiseled expanse of his massive chest. He couldn't look away from the awed expression on her lovely face as she focused on the way his pects flexed beneath her touch. He cupped her chin and kissed her deeply, his hips mimicking the thrusts of his tongue as he relaxed atop her writhing form. He was more than a little concerned about crushing her, but County was determined to feel every inch of him. Her fingers disappeared beneath the waistband of his sweats as she sought to tug them down.

"Contessa," he warned.

"This isn't fair," she moaned, shamelessly grinding herself against the incredible erection nudging her body.

Fernando grinned. "Serves you right for keeping me waiting all this time to have you again."

"Then punish me by showing me what I've been missing."

Her words threw his arousal into overdrive and together they tugged away the last of his clothing.

Fernando reached beneath one of the coral silk throw pillows littering the bed and extracted a condom. Once the protection was in place, he drew her against him and invaded her body with the iron proof of his desire.

Contessa's nails left tiny red half moon impressions upon his caramel skin. She cried out and arched into the fierce lunges. She was as pleasured by the sensation of his overwhelming size as she was by the way his muscles flexed and glistened from his exertions. A powerful climax racked her body when he pulled both her legs across his shoulders and increased penetration ten-fold.

Wanting more, he let her legs ease down and recaptured her wrists. Her hands pinned to the bed again, thrusting her breasts prominently upon her chest. Fernando was there to capture one nipple. His perfect teeth grazed the rigid bud, applying slight pressure until she cried out softly. Slowly, he alternated between suckling and bathing the nipple with his tongue.

County arched up to meet his slow, intense thrusts. Indecipherable words of delight tumbled past her lips only to be silenced when Fernando kissed her again. He brought her to orgasm more than once with his expert skills. County at times begged him to stop while she was in the throes of an extreme climax. Fernando delighted in torturing her with deeper thrusts as she screamed her fulfillment...

Afterward, Contessa could barely keep her eyes open. She was completely surrounded by Fernando—captive within his unyielding form. She could feel his heart beating against her back and willed herself not to fall asleep and be robbed of the memory of such a perfect feeling of contentment and security.

"I know I rushed you. I'm sorry."

His voice vibrated through her and County shook her head against a pillow. "It was no more than I rushed you," she said, "I wouldn't expect you to believe that I'd never done that before in my life. I've never taken a man home like that," she explained in a quiet voice.

Fernando grinned devilishly and kissed her shoulder. "I feel honored."

"I felt the complete opposite."

"Hey," he whispered, turning her over so that he could stare into her eyes. "Do you regret what happened?"

County looked around the room. "Not this—not us at this very moment, but before… Before I regretted it very much."

"Count—"

"It was enjoyable, but in doing it I think it may've seriously affected your ability to respect me," she grimaced, "not that you're looking for a woman to respect."

Fernando bowed his head in an attempt to hide his smile. He knew she was trying to protect herself— still. How could he get her to believe his feelings were turning down the same road as hers? *Patience man, she's yours, don't worry. Give her a chance. Give yourself a chance.*

"I'm sorry," County said, tugging her bottom lip between her teeth and fixing him with a wary look.

"I didn't mean to dampen the moment. It's just that I've been wanting to say that since the day we had lunch at Marvin's."

Making her lie flat on her back, Fernando leaned close and kissed the end of her nose. "You're my equal, don't you know that? If I'm going to feel you're unworthy of my respect because you let me come home with you, then I'd have to feel the same way about myself and I don't. Not one bit."

"But, I shouldn't have just taken you home for sex."

"Didn't you want it?"

"Yes, but—"

"So did I. I wanted it very much," he swore, taking the hand she nervously raked through her sleek, short cut, "But for the tenth time, it's not all I want. You have to know that Contessa."

She did know, she realized, watching her hand hidden within his. After all, they'd crossed the threshold into the lover's realm long before that night and he was still there, right? *Let him in County. Just a little. Give him a piece of your heart and if it feels right, give him more.*

"County? You okay?"

She nodded, smiling up into his probing brown eyes.

"Then let's eat," Fernando decided, preparing to carry her out of bed.

"Wait," she whispered, squeezing his biceps as she resisted. "Not just yet?" she suggested.

Fernando had no argument.

Chapter 6

"**B**ig Den!" Stefan greeted as he shook hands and hugged the tall, rotund man who entered his office that Monday morning.

Denmark Harrison grinned as well, though a trace of unease rested in his hazel gaze. "Smilin' Stef. Always happy," he teased lightly.

Stef rubbed his hands together. "Especially happy today, my man. Let's see what'cha got."

"Man, I gotta tell you, I don't feel so right about this," Denmark shared, clutching the tan envelope he seemed unwilling to let go of.

Stef maintained his smile and patted Den's elbow assuringly. "It's harmless," he promised.

"Maybe, but I don't feel right spying on Fern."

Stefan glanced at the bulging envelope. "You felt right enough to take a crapload of pictures. But then, twenty bucks a shot is quite a sale."

Denmark's uncertain stare turned cold and he passed the envelope to Stef.

His smirk still in place, Stef browsed through the photographs. His brows rose, not because there was anything rude or degrading in the collection. This was a Fernando Ramsey Stefan didn't know. This was Fernando Ramsey sweeping a woman off her feet. There were pictures showing the two of them out and about all over Chicago. Judging by the shots, he'd taken her out dancing, to jazz shows, R & B concerts...

"This a yacht?" he asked Den.

"A restaurant," the man explained. "It was hard getting a shot. Seems he had the owner shut the place down for himself and the lady."

"Life of the Ramseys," Stef sighed, his gaze narrowing with a touch of envy and spite. "He loves her," he noted, after shuffling through a few more of the pictures. Not quite believing the discovery, he quickly observed the remaining shots. Absently, he reached on his desk for a white envelope and passed it to Denmark.

"What's this all about, Stef?" Den asked after the payment was safely tucked away in his jacket.

"Thanks Den. We're done here," Stef replied,

coolly dismissing the man without a glance in his direction.

Alone in the office, Stefan splayed the pictures on his bar and studied them more closely. Fernando Ramsey was the very last man he ever pictured falling in love. Hell, he figured it'd happen to himself before his brooding partner. Of course, he could very well understand the attraction. Contessa Warren was most definitely a knockout. She was also business, Stef noted, his dark face tightening. He knew she had to be the reason Fernando instructed Anson and Graham to back away from the meeting.

Could there be more to it? He considered, taking a cigar from the silver case on the windowsill. Could his partner simply be turning up the charm? Was he trying to woo the lovely Ms. Warren into selling her publishing house? That had to be it! Sure she was a beauty and trust Fern to be enjoying every inch of her, Stef mused, grinning as he clipped the end off his cigar. Persuasion was such a dirty business, he chuckled.

Feeling a little more at ease, Stef buzzed Sheila at her desk. "Fernando in yet?" he asked, when she picked up his call.

"Not yet, Stefan. He did call to say he'd taken a later flight out of Chicago. Said he should be in a little after one."

"No rush," Stef drawled, lighting the fat cigar.

"Just let him know I want to see him when he gets here." Satisfied, Stef ended the call and settled down to review the photos again.

Tykira's laughter filled the living room as her husband placed her on the sofa. "Your neighbors are going to think you've gone crazy. You're always carrying me inside this place!"

Quay shrugged. "This time it's for tradition," he excused.

Ty's look was playfully skeptical. "I don't know, every woman who lives here is gonna be after her man to do the same."

"Tough. A woman should be carried every now and then," he decided, smoothing his hands across her jean clad thighs. "Especially if she's you," he added, leaning close to ply her neck with kisses.

Ty smiled contentedly and cupped the back of his head. When Quay's innocent kisses traveled to the opening of her blouse, she sobered. "So what do you want to do today?" she asked.

"I'm doin' it," he growled, his lips grazing the tops of her breasts.

"Quay, be serious. I'm talking about work."

"No problem," he said, moving to relax next to her on the sofa, "I can wait for you to handle your business."

Ty pushed back a curl that had tumbled from her upswept hairstyle. "Not my business. *Yours.*"

Quay waved one hand, his eyes were closed. "Q has it covered for a little while longer."

Ty knew this was going to be unpleasant, but felt she had to try. "Sweetie, what about the rest of your family?" she inquired, wincing when she saw the muscle flex in his jaw. "I know you don't want to discuss it," she called when he bolted from the sofa, "but you've got me worried. You're acting like they don't exist."

Quay poured a cooler glass full of gin, downed it and prepared another.

"You're gonna have to face this thing sooner or later," she said when he was halfway through the second glass. When he slammed it down on the bar, she shook her head.

"You know what's goin' on here, Tyke," he muttered.

"And I'm sorry, but I don't want this between us and it will be as long as we're here in Seattle."

Quay drained the glass. "We don't have to be in Seattle."

Stunned, Ty searched his onyx gaze for some hint that he was teasing. She found no such hint. "What about your business? My mom? Your family? Baby, I can see us making a life here."

"Seeing my family makes me think about all the time I spent without you."

She scooted to the edge of the black suede sofa. "Quay—"

"No Tyke," he urged, raising his hand as he stepped from behind the bar, "it wasn't a good time. I tried to make it a good time, had everyone convinced," he shared with a right dimpled grin that faded momentarily. "I had everyone convinced but myself. I don't want to go back to that."

Ty left the sofa and went over to pull him into a tight hug. "But you won't. I'm here and I'm not going anywhere," she vowed, kissing his ear when he buried his face in her neck. "Quay?" she whispered, once they'd stood silent in the embrace for a time.

"Hmm?" he grunted.

"Whether we're here or not, there may come a time when we'll run into Marc or Houston. What happens when we do?" she wondered, feeling his arms tighten about her waist.

"Tyke, I honestly don't know."

"County? Can I see you a minute, please?"

Contessa braced herself when she heard Spivey's voice. She knew she was about to hear something she really didn't want to. Over the last several weeks, her research crew had uncovered several interesting tidbits on many of the Ramseys. Many had speculated there could possibly be enough material for an engrossing novel on each family member.

"Yeah?" she said, turning to favor Spivey with a smile. She preceded him to his office door and folded her arms across her chest. "Do I have to guess?" she prompted, when Spivey stood grinning for at least five seconds.

"We may have something very interesting going on with the Ramseys right here in our own backyard," he shared.

County waved her hand, motioning for him to continue.

"I have a friend who's a gofer at The Spot for one of the managers there," he said, moving past County to take a seat behind his desk. "He told me they've been having problems with girls disappearing."

"Disappearing?" County asked, shaking her head for clarification.

"Since before the beginning of the year," Spivey said, shuffling through the contents of a folder, "girls have been leaving the club in a steady stream. It's picked up even more in the last month."

County shrugged. "What's so special about that? Have they been abducted or something?"

"It's not that. According to my friend they've found new jobs."

"Again Spivey, I don't see why that's a big deal," she said, hiding her hands in the pockets of her gray pin-striped trousers, "You know, stripping and prostitution aren't exactly what most girls dream of doing when they grow up."

Spivey nodded to concede her point. "But it could be a tough business to leave. Know what I mean?" he challenged.

"Well, does your contact know where the girls are working?"

Spivey's attractive brown face reflected disappointment. "Trail goes cold there. But my boy did say the managers had a big meeting last week—closed session. Says he's gonna keep checking for me."

"Right…"

"County? Um…are you sure you want me to keep looking?"

She blinked, not bothering to hide the fact that the question surprised as much as it embarrassed her. "Why wouldn't I?" she asked, knowing full well he was referring to her very public relationship with the club's owner.

Spivey studied his boss, taking in the determined look in her eyes. It was a look he knew well and one that gave a clear answer to his question. He nodded. "Just checking," he told her.

County tugged on the cuffs of the white blouse that peeked from the sleeves of her gray blazer. "Come see me when you've got more," she instructed, then left his office.

In the hall, she dropped the mask and let her unease fall into place. She and Fernando Ramsey had become more than lovers. He was becoming so dear to her as a friend—a relationship she really didn't think could exist with a man who was a lover. What if Spivey uncovered something damaging?

Grimacing at the thought, she punched her palm
with a balled fist. This was business and it should be
her first and only consideration. The only problem
was her first and only consideration was taking a
backseat to the man she believed she was falling in
love with.

"But isn't it a little too soon to tell?" Mick asked,
nervously twirling a curly lock around her finger as
she spoke with her obstetrician.

"It's *exactly* the time," Dr. Georgian Steins
informed his patient.

"I see."

Clearing his throat, Dr. Steins debated on his next
words. "We could always keep the ultrasound results
for the baby's sex a secret," he proposed, sensing her
hesitation, "if you and Quest would like for it to be
a surprise."

"Quest," Mick said, blinking as her husband came
to mind, "I have no idea whether he wants to know
or not. I—I haven't even told him about the ultrasound I—um—I don't know what he'll say," she
uttered a nervous laugh. "I suppose I should've
already asked."

Dr. Steins chuckled as well. "Michaela, don't be
so hard on yourself. I guarantee you'll let many things
slip your mind in the coming weeks. A huge change
is about to take place in your life," he cautioned, taking
her off-kilter behavior as signs of mother-to-be angst.

"Thanks Dr. Steins, I'll talk with you later today," Mick said, not bothering to tell him her attitude had to do with a lot more than being scatterbrained. She wrapped up the call in time to hear her husband bellowing her name.

"In the den, Quest!" she called, waiting for his steps to draw closer before she put a dazzling smile in place.

Quest didn't waste time with verbal greetings. The look on his gorgeous molasses-toned face was determined as he crossed the den and pulled her close. Mick gave a breathless moan when he captured her mouth in a possessive kiss. She responded eagerly thrusting her tongue against his out of sheer desire.

"When do you have to be back?" she gasped when he released her mouth to shower her jaw with kisses.

"I don't," he growled. Then, as though he somehow sensed her mood, he drew away to observe her. "Tell me what's wrong," he said.

Mick didn't bother to deny it. "I just spoke with Dr. Steins. He wants to set a date for the ultrasound. I didn't know if you could be there."

"You just tell me when it is and I'll be there," he said, leaning in to kiss the mole at the corner of her mouth.

"Um, he also said we could find out the baby's sex."

Quest's brows rose in surprise. "Already?" he asked.

Mick smiled. "I was surprised too, but Dr. Steins says he should be able to tell. But he also said it could be a surprise," she added quickly and clasped her hands against his wide chest. "We don't have to know until the baby comes."

Quest shook his head. "I don't think I can wait that long," he said and witnessed Mick's crestfallen reaction. "What? Do you want to wait?"

She gave a quick toss of her head and tried to appear refreshed. "Whatever you want," she said.

"Uh-uh. What's going on?"

"Quest…"

"I'm listening."

"It's stupid."

"I'm getting used to it," he teased, feigning discomfort when she smacked his forehead. "Tell me," he urged while leading her to one of the ladder-backed bar stools in the den.

"I'm afraid to know," she blurted, unable to resist the persuasive power of his gray black stare.

"Why?" he whispered, rubbing the sides of her thighs.

Mick squeezed her eyes closed and buried her face in her hands. "I've been so worried that I wouldn't do right by it. Referring to the baby as 'it' somehow makes it easier to handle than saying him or her." She met her husband's gaze. "I'm bringing another person into the world, Quest. One who's gonna depend on me for everything. It's gonna be so helpless—how will I know if I'm doing right where it's concerned?"

"Baby," he soothed, pressing a kiss to the middle of her curls. "Hell yeah, you're gonna do right by it."

"How can you be so sure?" Mick challenged, searching his face as though the answer may be forthcoming. "A person usually does what they know. All I know is hurt and loss."

"Don't do this to yourself," he soothed, kissing her cheeks and forehead.

Mick smiled and stroked the curve of his jaw. "You're so sweet and I'll be fine. I promise," she whispered and leaned in to hug him. The lost expression still clouded her face as Quest's face harbored the same look.

"Hey man, Sheila said you wanted to see me when I got back," Fernando called out to his partner.

Stef looked up, grinning when he saw the man standing in his office doorway. "Good weekend?" he inquired.

"Damn good."

"Where the hell you runnin' off to every Friday, man?" Stef inquired as he stood.

"People to see," Fernando replied coolly, punctuating the remark with a lazy shrug. "So what's up? Why'd you want to see me?"

"Damn man, what's the hurry?"

"You mean besides all the work on my desk?"

Fernando challenged sarcastically. In truth, his thoughts were only focused on a particular box of files which he'd avoided going through since acquiring it two months earlier.

"Well, I'll get right to it then," Stef sighed, coming to perch on the edge of his desk. "You got any new ideas for the Contessa House deal?"

Frowning now, Fernando strolled past the doorway. "What do you mean, new ideas?"

Stef's look was innocent. "Clearly the owner's tough on the subject of selling. It's gonna take a lot to convince her. The deal is a very good one and she's still holding out. Perhaps we can come up with a few, um, creative ways to be more *persuasive?*" he suggested, knowing Fernando was not pleased by his insinuation. Still, he had to know just how against the deal he was.

"I want all negotiations ceased against that House," Fernando simply and firmly instructed.

"Whoa, Fern now maybe you've forgotten how lucrative—"

"I mean it Stef. Let it go."

"What made you change your mind all of a sudden?"

Fernando's caramel-toned face was rigid in the wake of a rising temper. "I changed my mind a long time ago," he shared.

Stef stroked his jaw and asked why.

"She doesn't want to sell," Fernando told his partner, sounding as though the fact was apparent.

Stefan was not convinced. "And?" he retorted, focusing on a spot at the end of his silk cobalt tie. "Never stopped you before."

"That was before."

"Fern—"

"Stef, drop it."

Observing his partner and conceding the unspoken fact that Fernando's word was final, Stef decided to let it go. For the time. "So then tell me about this trip, man."

"It was a trip, man," Fernando whispered, his tone signifying more details would not be included.

Stef's brows rose and he decided to let the subject slide as well. "So what about your schedule for today or is that off-limits, too?"

The question took Fernando's thoughts back to the box that sat waiting for him in his office. "I got some digging around to do. It's about my father."

Stef was heading back behind his desk. "Helping him out?" he figured.

"Investigating him."

"What?" Stef asked, his eyes locking with Fernando's. "Investigating your own father? Since when? Why?"

Fernando rubbed his fingers through his crop of brown curls and shook his head. "I can't believe it either, but it has to be done."

"Why man?" Stef asked again, bracing both hands upon his desktop as he leaned forward.

"You know about my uncle Houston?" he asked, watching his friend nod. "Well, the fact that we only suspect my pops of helping to keep him out of sight is only the tip of the iceberg. We think he's done much worse. Somethin' has to be done to get him away from the family—before anything more comes out," he added, easing one hand into the pocket of his blackberry trousers as he watched the view past the windows.

"You sure there's more?" Stef asked, fixing Fernando with a wary stare.

"I'm sure of it," he answered without hesitation. "I just hope I'm about to get some answers."

Stef waited a moment, and then walked over and clapped Fernando's shoulder. "You're a brave man, kid. I wouldn't have the nerve to dig into my father's business."

Fernando acknowledged silently that he didn't have the nerve, either. Unfortunately, this had waited for too long.

Chapter 7

"How long do you think you'll be able to hide him?" Cufi Muhammad asked his friend.

Marc groaned and massaged his eyes. "I don't think it can play out much longer and having him out there with you was my best idea."

"Maybe it's time for you to let your brother go. Know what I mean?"

Marc's grin was humorless. "I know exactly what you mean and don't think I haven't thought of that very thing."

"But?"

"As my oldest friend, you know better than anyone why I can't do that."

"Do you think Houston has the nerve to bring you down with him?" Cufi asked in an incredulous tone.

"Hell, I've helped him to elude the police going on three months! Among other things…"

"Among other things…" Cufi repeated the phrase as though he were contemplating.

Marc's brows drew close. "Care to share what you're thinkin' man?"

"Do you think anyone would believe Houston if he decided to tell what he knows, my friend?"

"My family would, that's for damn sure," Marc acknowledged with a weary smile. "Hell, if I don't have my own family on my side, how can I expect anyone else would stand there?"

"It may be possible if no one took Houston's ravings as fact," Cufi said after several moments of silence.

"Ravings?" Marc repeated.

"Mmm. Given the nature of his crime—a crime that has occurred more than once unbeknownst to the authorities at this time. Not to mention the man's penchant for flying off the handle."

"Hold it Cufi," Marc urged, sitting straighter in his desk chair, "are you suggesting we try to prove he's crazy?"

"I think it'd be rather easy."

"He's my brother," Marc noted, swallowing down unexpected emotion.

Cufi's chuckle harbored no humor. "Look at it

from a humane perspective, friend. Houston was only wanted for questioning, but he ran. That in itself gives the hard impression of guilt. The physical evidence proves he was with Sera that night. She was a minor at the time. Clearly he's going down, but with an insanity defense the time he serves may not be so hard."

"That's absurd!" Marc blurted, bursting into laughter as he did so. "Besides, pleading insanity is the one defense black folks don't have a chance in hell of proving."

"Why not?"

"For one thing, we're not white."

Cufi laughed. "A minor detail when all others are in place."

"Such as?"

"Extreme wealth, power, notoriety. Your family can trace its roots back to the motherland and in America—to the Georgia plantation you worked as slaves. Besides," Cufi added as though he were sharing a closely guarded secret, "you know the black community doesn't call attention to mental deficiencies as quickly as other races—it's something we do our best to ignore. All these things could play in your favor, my friend."

Marc was silent, contemplating Cufi's points for a while. At last, he began to nod slowly. "So how exactly would we go about making this happen?"

* * *

"What'cha got?" County asked Spivey and Jenean as she reclined in her desk chair.

"My contact at the club is on his game," Spivey commended, when Jenean waved for him to begin, "it turns out that the girls are working for a local travel agency."

Folding her arms across her scoop-necked mauve top, County fixed Jenean with a pointed look. "What's so odd about that?"

"As hostesses."

"That *is* odd," Jenean noted.

"Indeed," County confirmed, one because these were former strippers. Though it wasn't always the case, stripping and prostitution went hand in hand. Therefore, "hostess" was a job title with many connotations.

"What would a travel agency need with hostesses?" County mused.

"You want us to stay on it?" Spivey asked, after they'd sat in silence a little over two minutes.

County, however, was in another world. Her gaze was steady and determined, but clearly she was focused on something or someone else.

"County? Contessa…?"

"I'm sorry?" County blinked, focusing on Spivey and Jenean. Clearing her throat, she nodded. "Stay on it," she instructed, offering a wavering smile when they stood and left her office.

Alone, County chewed her thumbnail and debated. She could only think of Fernando and their weekend together—all their weekends together. Their time had been so sweet. Now she questioned the intelligence of digging into his business. What if this—she and Fernando—was something to last? Would her actions come back to haunt her? She was falling for him. *Falling?* Ha! She'd *fallen*—hard, fast and quite willingly. He was absolutely the last kind of man she ever envisioned losing her heart to. He was far from a pushover, not in the least intimidated by her strength or accomplishments; he wouldn't let her push him away with some weak reason. In essence, he was her equal and she was his. Now she was betraying him…

"Dammit!" she hissed, with a shake of her head. She was making too much of this. She decided then that there was no harm in digging a little deeper, if for no other reason than to satisfy her own curiosity. *All right County, if that helps you sleep tonight.*

The phone buzzed and she welcomed the interruption. "Yeah Monica?"

"Stefan Lyons for you County."

"Lyons?" she parroted, not recognizing the name her assistant gave.

"Of Dark Squires Communications," Monica added.

"Ahh…" County sighed, scratching the arch of

her brow as realization set in. "Send him through Mon," she said, finding herself eager to hear what this next pitch would entail.

"Ms. Warren, Stefan Lyons, co-founder of Dark Squires."

"Mr. Lyons, I'm both pleased and flattered to be speaking with the top man."

Stefan chuckled on his end. "I always consider it a necessity to speak with potential clients who break down my best salesmen."

"Mmm, again I'm flattered. And you have wonderful salesmen, but I have no desire or intention to sell my House."

"Clearly," Stef replied, his voice losing a trace of its lightness. "Still, I'm hoping to work this out. Surely there must be some improvements we could make to the deal that would be more encouraging to you?"

"There are no improvements, Mr. Lyons. My mind is made up, my decision is final."

"You don't seem to understand what Dark Squires can offer."

"And you don't seem to understand that you're wasting your time."

"You're a small house, we can make you bigger *and* better."

"Bigger, perhaps," County conceded with a smirk. "Better, I seriously doubt."

Finally, Stef expelled a muttered curse. "You're a fool."

"Excuse me—"

"Excuse me," Stef countered, "what I should've said is 'you're a woman'."

"You—"

"Clearly, you're ruled by your emotions. A sentimental need to hold on to your *baby.* A real businessman would want his baby to grow and become a challenge in this industry."

County's lashes fluttered, she was so riled. "*Clearly,* business is your strong suit, Mr. Lyons. I'm willing to bet you've got no real experience in publishing. Creative thinking, passion *and* emotion are just as important. If not, more so."

"You're letting a once in a lifetime opportunity slip right through your fingers."

"I truly doubt that," County sneered, sitting on the corner of her desk and enjoying the chance to run down the pompous business*man* on the other end of the line.

"You huge conglomerates are a dime a dozen. Another will be sniffing 'round my doorstep before the close of business today. You bastards zero in and swoop down on independents like vultures. Still, in defense of the others, I'm sure they don't resort to bullying and name calling when the owners are content on not selling."

"Ms. Warren—"

"Call me again with this bull, write me a letter or dammit send me an e-mail that even *hints* about selling and you'll find the *good* name of Dark Squires Communications looking like it just took a good roll in the mud. And I don't threaten. I guarantee."

Stef actually jumped when the phone slammed down in his ear. His jaw was clenched tight in anger and he could do no more than ball his fists and pray for calm.

"Finally getting around to that box, eh?" Kathy Hughes teased her boss when she came to get his signature on a few documents.

Fernando laughed. "I couldn't stand it taking up space in that corner for another week," he admitted, casting a forlorn look toward that area of his office.

"Well, I'll leave you to your fun once I get you to sign these requisitions."

"Thanks Kat," Fernando said as he applied the last signature. Alone in his office, he groaned and shuffled through a few more papers. He'd been at it a little over an hour and nothing had struck him as odd. Not one thing. That could mean only *two* things: Marcus had covered his tracks very well or there was nothing to find. Fernando was willing to bet it was more of the former.

In truth, he wasn't waiting on pins and needles to find something to destroy Marc. After all, the man was his father. But Josephine was his mother and he'd seen Marc wear her down to a shell during the sentence of her marriage to him. Then there was Yohan and Melina and Houston's murder of Sera Black...

"Come on, man," he urged, running all ten fingers through his brown curls and attempting to focus.

Besides, the box and all its contents had to be returned by the end of the month. He'd scoured his father's office thoroughly following his banishment from Ramsey Enterprises. The board was now trying to decide whether his absence would be permanent or if there was still a place for him in the family business. Meanwhile, Marc was handling his affairs from either home or the private office he kept in downtown Seattle.

Idly now, Fernando rifled through more papers until something caught his eye. "What's this?" he murmured, his long brows drawing close. Then a smile curved his mouth when he discovered the document was an e-mail from his father's "sent" file.

"I'll be damned," Fernando sighed, leaning back in his desk chair. He recalled a conversation where he'd chided Marc for printing copies and reminded the man that was what a "sent" file was for.

Marc coolly replied that systems break down and files could be lost or corrupted. *A hard copy is forever,* he said. Fernando remembered chalking it up to the fact that his dad just didn't trust anything or anyone. *That too,* Marc confessed.

Now, Fernando celebrated his father's suspicious nature. The page he held appeared quite interesting. It was a request from Marcus to his business attorney Shawn Givens. Marc was asking the man to get the ball rolling on a transfer of ownership for *The Wind Rage*. Simple enough, but it left Fernando with two questions: What was *The Wind Rage* and why was his father requesting that its ownership be transferred to him? His first inclination was to dial Shawn Givens, but that wouldn't be wise, he decided. Then, he had a better thought and dialed a different number.

His eyes crinkled in their usual manner when he smiled at the sound of his mother's voice.

"This is quite a surprise!" Josephine cried, delighted to hear from her middle son.

"You act like I never call," Fernando said, actually a little upset by the fact.

"Oh, you," Josephine sighed over the line, "you know it's a rarity for you to call me in the middle of the day like this."

Fernando pressed a hand to the middle of his chest. "Are you deliberately tryin' to make me feel like a low-down son?"

Josephine laughed. "Not low-down, just one who should call more."

"Thanks."

"And in light of that, I should ask when we'll see each other again?"

"I'll come over tonight."

"Tonight? You mean you aren't taking another trip?"

Fernando grinned. "Not tonight, Ma."

"That's right," Josephine whispered as though she were just realizing, "these trips usually take place over the weekends."

"Ma…" Fernando groaned, knowing where her probes were headed.

"Dare I suggest that these are weekend…getaways?"

"Would you believe it's business?"

"Not in a million years. What's her name?"

Fernando debated, stroking his jaw as he hesitated on answering. "Mick's friend. Contessa Warren," he revealed finally.

"Ahh…the publisher."

"That's right and Ma please don't lecture me, all right?"

"Lecture you about what? I think the girl has spunk like Mick and Ty…and Mel."

Fernando was silent, hearing the sadness in his mother's voice when she spoke of Yohan's estranged wife.

"The family needs more women like them. Not fools who let themselves get run over by conniving bastards."

Knowing exactly who his mother meant, Fernando cleared his throat and decided it was the perfect time to introduce the reason for his call. "Ma, what can you tell me about *The Wind Rage?* You ever hear Pop mention it?"

"What? His boat?"

"Boat?"

Josephine muttered something inaudible. "Excuse me, *ship,*" she clarified. "Your father always got on me for referring to that thing as a boat."

"Well, um, what sort of ship is it?" he asked, his brows drawn close in expectation.

"I don't really know, baby. I always thought it was some cargo ship for Ramsey. I'd never seen it, only heard about it."

"When did Pop buy it?"

"About seven years after we were married," Josephine said, a twinge of disgust coloring her words, "he didn't own it outright, just went in with about four friends. Sweetie, why are you so interested in this?"

"Because it's mine," Fernando shared without hesitation.

"Yours?" Josephine gasped.

"Mmm," Fernando confirmed, a smirk souring his handsome features. "For the life of me, I can't see why he'd hand somethin' like that over to me."

"Must be going bankrupt because that's the only reason that fool would *give* anything away. What'd he'd say when he gave it to you?"

Fernando shook his head. "He didn't tell me about it. I found out on my own."

"Honey what's going on?"

Reaching for the e-mail, Fernando's translucent brown gaze held no trace of its usual warmth. "I don't know Ma, but I'm damn well gonna find out."

"Why didn't you tell me you were stopping by?" Mick laughed, while pulling her mother-in-law into a hug. "I would've started lunch if I'd known."

"Please," Catrina said with a wave, "you know I wouldn't hear of it. I've been meaning to stop by and check on you for a while now."

"Well, I'm fine," Mick said as they strolled out of the foyer, arms linked around one another's waists. "What'll you have?" she called, once they entered the living room and she headed toward the bar.

"That looks good," Catrina noted, referring to the tall glass of apple juice Mick was preparing. "Make it two," she requested.

"You got it," Mick said.

"So…is everything *really* all right?" Catrina asked, after watching her daughter-in-law for a while.

Mick crossed the room, carrying the apple juice and wearing a knowing smile on her round, dark face. "Did Quest ask you to come over here?"

"Quest?" Catrina parroted from her relaxed position on the sofa. "I told you I'd been planning to visit for quite some time."

"Mmm…" Mick replied, sipping her juice and fixing Catrina with a stern look.

The woman broke finally. "He's very concerned, honey."

"You can tell your son that I'm fine," Mick requested in a pouting manner.

"*You* can tell *him* that," Catrina decided, watching the juice swirl amidst the ice cubes inside her glass. "I want you to tell *me* the truth."

"Catrina—"

"The truth," she insisted, setting the glass aside and leaning forward. "Whatever it is, it stays between the two of us."

Setting aside her glass as well, Mick braced her elbows to her knees. "I want this baby so much," she swore, pushing back her unruly curls with her fingers. "I want to be a great mother, a great role model."

A frown tugged at Catrina's arched brows. "Sweetie of course you'll be those things."

"Then why am I scared to death that I won't be?" Mick blurted, allowing the fear to shine in her amber gaze.

"Oh…" Catrina soothed, moving close to hold Mick as she cried. "It's all right, it's all right…" she chanted, knowing the younger woman's cry was long overdue.

"Please don't tell Quest," Mick begged once her tears were spent. "He's so on edge because of me. He jumps every time I stand up."

Catrina laughed. "Sweetie, he's just a nervous, expectant father."

"Which is why he sent you," Mick noted, searching Catrina's eyes for any trace of denial. "All right then," she sighed, slapping her hands to the cotton fabric of her sky blue sweats, "lay it on me. Tell me I'm overreacting, that this is all expectant mother stuff."

Catrina smiled and made a little room between herself and Mick. "Your fears are perfectly understandable," she acknowledged, stoking Mick's curls in a reassuring way. "Baby, your life hasn't been easy. The things you've been through...of course, you'd feel this way."

"Then how will I know what's best for it? How will I know what to do?" she asked, swallowing down more sobs.

Catrina fixed her with a sympathetic albeit amused smile. "Sweetie, I hate to tell you this. But, the sad truth is that you won't really know a damn thing."

"Thanks."

"Now, now," Catrina soothed, patting Mick's damp cheek, "it's the same with every parent regardless of their upbringing. But there *is* one thing you can count on and if you put your trust in that, the rest will fall into place."

"What?" Mick blurted, her eyes widening with hope and expectation. "Catrina, what?" she cried, clasping her hands to her chest.

"What's in here," Catrina asked, pressing

Michaela's hands closer to her chest. "Trust in the
love you feel for this tiny man or woman. Love your
child. Trust your instincts," she said, tapping Mick's
chin with her index finger. "You've got wonderful instincts and ethics and they're all *yours,* not your
mother's. So stop being so hard on yourself, all
right?"

Mick's shoulders slumped as though she'd been
relieved of some tremendous weight. Love her
child? She did—so much and she hadn't even met
him or her yet. Trust her instincts? She knew she'd
give her life to protect its own.

"That really *is* all I need to know," she whispered,
shaking her head in disbelief.

Catrina laughed. "Well, what are you doing
now?" she called, watching Mick race to the phone
and begin dialing furiously.

"I'm calling Quest! We've got a doctor's appointment to keep!"

"Pay dirt!" Spivey announced when he burst into
Contessa's office late that afternoon.

"Aw Spivey, can't it wait?" Contessa whined,
massaging her tired eyes as she spoke. "It's been a
very long day."

"Not a chance. I found out where the dancers
are working."

County rolled her eyes. "I thought we knew that
already? This travel agency."

"Mmm-hmm," Spivey confirmed, perching on the edge of his boss's desk. "The agency hired the girls as hostesses for a cruise ship."

Slightly intrigued, County remained silent and waited for her editor to continue.

"My contact got this on good authority from one of the secretarys at the agency."

"Are you sure you can trust this guy?"

A grin broke on Spivey's handsome vanilla-toned face. "For the money I'm payin' him, I'm sure of it."

"Hmph." County shrugged, relief filling her at the discovery that there wasn't more to the story. "Well, I'm sorry you hit a dead end, but we've spent long enough on this and we've got more than enough to move on."

"But County wait. I haven't reached a dead end." Spivey corrected, waving his hand as he rounded the desk. "This isn't just some fun in the sun cruise ship. It's some sort of gentlemen-only thing."

The sinking feeling in the pit of her stomach warned Contessa that she wouldn't care for the rest of Spivey's report. "Why would it—uh—need to be a *gentlmen-only* ship?" she inquired cautiously.

Spivey's expression was one of sheer cunning. "Baby if we knew the answer to that, I believe we could blow some big names out of the water. All we have so far, is that gambling's involved. Beyond that, no idea," he said, clasping his hands while he shrugged beneath his green pin-striped suit.

"Beyond that…" County sighed, massaging the sudden tension tightening her neck. "Gambling and possibly prostitution on the high seas? What more could a guy want?"

"How 'bout the name of one of the ship's owners?" Spivey announced, watching County's eyes narrow. "Fernando Ramsey," he said.

Chapter 8

His voice brought on that familiar shiver down her spine and an instant later she was fluffing her hair. She made sure her lipstick was perfect. Standing was best, she decided, and chose to pretend to scan a file instead of sitting primly behind her desk.

Fernando's voice lowered and Sheila pouted, knowing he'd stopped to take a few extra moments to speak with someone. Then, she heard him biding them farewell and her heart pounded wildly in anticipation of seeing him.

"What's goin' on Sheila? You doin' all right?" Fernando greeted, having no idea of the effect of his entrancing smile and deliciously deep voice.

"Morning! Morning Fernando," she spoke softer that time.

Fernando, of course, had no idea his partner's secretary felt anything other than respect and friendliness toward him. He'd be a shabby businessman if he allowed the adoration of every woman who worked for Dark Squires to go to his head.

"Stef in?" Fernando asked, pausing just past Sheila's desk.

"Just stepped out Fernando. Sorry," she whispered, though her eyes continued to sparkle. "Could I take a message?" she added hastily, realizing she'd been staring.

Fernando grimaced. "I really wanted to speak with him today," he said, casting an impatient glance toward Stefan's door at the end of the hall. "Any idea when he'll be back?"

"I have no idea," Sheila said, her tone soft and apologetic as she rounded her desk, "is anything wrong?"

"Nah, I'm on my way out of town."

It was clear to see that Fernando was quite pleased over the fact and Sheila felt her confidence dwindle a little. "Off to Chicago again?" she guessed.

"That's right," he shared, the grin on his face practically shouted that this trip had nothing to do with business. "Look, just tell Stef I'll call," he said and leaned over to press a quick kiss to Sheila's cheek. "Thanks."

Sheila stood there next to her desk, her eyes following Fernando as he made his way down the hallway. "Anytime." She almost swooned and brushed her fingers across her cheek where he'd kissed her.

Standing quietly in a hidden corner of the hallway, Stef took in the sweet scene. A deadly look darkened his face as he studied Sheila's reaction to his partner.

Tykira leaned over the black tiled counter and browsed one of the cookbooks she'd discovered in the kitchen.

Quay strolled in and appreciated the lovely scene greeting him. After satisfying himself by admiring the picture she made from behind, he slowly closed the distance between them.

Ty expressed a tiny shriek when she felt her husband's hands beneath the snug T-shirt she wore. The other disappeared below the waistband of the boy shorts she sported. "I'm trying to decide on dinner," she sang, clearing her throat when his fingers grazed the sensitive bud of her femininity.

"Forget dinner. I'll have you," Quay decided.

Tykira's laughter perched atop another gasp when his fingers found their destination. Her head fell forward as overwhelming sensation threaded throughout her body. She began to thrust madly against his fingers before turning in his arms. "Why do you need all these cookbooks when you never cook?" she asked as they shared a heated kiss.

"I bought them when you were here recovering, when you'd broken your ankle," Quay explained, his mouth now clinging to the line of her neck. "I thought I'd give it a try."

Ty pulled back a little to stare into his gorgeous dark face. "I thought you were just teasing when you told me you'd cook."

Quay pressed his forehead to hers. "Don't you know by now I'd do anything for you?"

Another kiss was in order, this one sweet and unhurried. Yet it lacked none of the fire. Quay cupped Ty's thighs and placed her neatly atop the counter, never breaking the kiss. The sound of a ringing phone was smothered amidst moans and words of desire. The couple had no intention of answering, knowing the machine would pick up by the fourth ring.

The fourth ring never sounded. The phone stopped ringing only to start up again seconds later. The pattern continued two more times, before Quay lost his patience and snatched the wall phone from its holder.

"Yeah?" he practically growled.

"Calm down," Michaela ordered, not at all affected by her brother-in-law's tone. "Why aren't you and Ty answering the phone?"

"One guess."

"Nasty."

"Look who's talkin'," Quay teased, chuckling softly when he heard Mick's haughty sniff.

"Listen, I promise not to hold you long. I'm just calling to remind you of the shower."

Quay bristled and stood. "This a family thing?" he asked.

"Of course it's a family thing."

"I'm out."

"*No*. You have to be there."

"Dammit Mick," Quay rolled his eyes. "I can't make it, that's all there is to it."

"Why can't you?" Mick snapped.

"Work," he tried.

"You're the boss," she countered.

"I'm a newlywed."

"And your wife's one of my hostesses, so she'll be at my house and not there for you to tie to the bed," Mick threw back, hearing the weary sigh he uttered. "Oh, honey, don't you want to know whether it'll be a little niece or nephew you'll have to spoil?"

"Quest'll tell me."

"I'll see to it that he doesn't."

Again, Quay groaned. "Damn you," he said after another minute or two.

Mick laughed. "May I take that as a yes?"

"Mmm-hmm," Quay grudgingly agreed after a moment.

"You promise?"

"Promise."

"Right, I'll speak with your wife now to tell her you've accepted."

Rolling his eyes, Quay pressed the phone to his chest and fixed Ty with a dark look. "Mick," he announced, passing her the phone.

Unfortunately, it was virtually impossible for Ty and Mick to hold a conversation. Quay began a sensuous assault with kisses to his wife's thigh, the moment she began to speak into the phone. Ty couldn't concentrate on a thing and could only promise Mick she'd get Quay there before the call ended.

"I expect you to get me out of this," he ordered, his voice muffled against her throat.

"You shouldn't have promised, then. Besides, don't you want to know about the baby?"

Quay fixed his wife with a narrowed stare. "Sure I do, but you know how I feel. This thing'll be a big disaster if I get there and see Marcus. He'd get everything I want to lay on Houston."

"Shh…" Ty soothed, brushing her fingertips along the furrows on his brow. "You shouldn't worry about that. Quest'll be there and he won't let you do anything and neither will I. Besides—" she shrugged and gave him a saucy wink "—you know Mick will kick your ass if you ruin her party."

Quay couldn't contain his laughter. "Damn right," he agreed.

"Are you okay now?" Ty asked, tilting her head

just a bit to gaze more steadily into his eyes as her fingers curled into the neckline of his white T-shirt.

He nodded. "I am."

Tykira sighed and glanced back at the cookbook she'd been studying. "So, what are we gonna do for dinner?"

The wolfish smile disappeared on Quay's face as he threaded his fingers through her tumbling tresses. "We're already doing it," he said and drew her into a satisfying kiss.

Contessa tugged on the lapels of her ankle-length leather trench and strolled off the elevator. Her gait was alluring and unhurried as always, but still she looked like a woman with a lot on her mind. She'd replayed her conversation with Spivey five times already and was always left with the same question: Why did Fernando own a cruise ship for gentlemen only? Of course, there was always the same answer: There was more going on than gambling. There had to be, right? She remembered when she'd questioned him about The Spot. She'd believed him and felt bad for doubting when he insisted there was nothing illegal afoot. But what about this? Should she ask him? Would the story be the same?

"Hey Drake," she greeted the evening security guard.

"Evening, Ms. Warren," Drake replied, turning around the log for her to sign out.

"Night," she whispered, leaving the middle-aged Haitian with a warm smile before turning toward the row of glass doors. Her steps slowed the closer she drew to the exit.

Asking him would be best, she decided. Just put all the damn cards on the table and let the chips fall. Would he fly off the handle? Would they argue and decide to end things? At least then she'd be free to handle her business without guilt. But then, she'd be without him.

"Are you hungry?"

The depth of his voice, riddled her spine with the most delicious sensation. Closing her eyes briefly, she rid her mind of unwelcomed thoughts before turning to greet him with a brilliant smile. "I'm starving," she told him.

Fernando's smile relayed curiosity as his vibrant brown eyes narrowed. "Are you referring to food?" he inquired softly.

"'Course I am!" County laughed.

A broad shoulder rose in a shrug. "Just checking." Fernando said, pretending as though he'd been confused.

They headed outside the building and into the biting cold. Fernando drew her close and Contessa wanted to snuggle into the warmth that radiated from his massive form.

"Damn, Chicago winters are as ferocious as its summers are gorgeous," he noted.

County smiled and blinked up at the darkened sky. "That's why I love it so—from one extreme to the next. Makes me feel alive," she praised.

Fernando ushered them inside the back of the waiting Mercedes limo. He turned to County and extended his hand. Familiar with the routine, she dropped her keys to his palm.

"James, take care of Ms. Warren's car after you drop us off," he instructed his driver.

"So, um, where are we going for dinner?" County asked, while removing her coat.

"We're here," Fernando announced, winking devilishly when she frowned her surprise.

County shook her head when she noticed him waving the bag which carried the logo of a well-known deli in town. "I can't believe you'd want to feast on messy subs in this car," she said, shaking misty rain from her chic cut.

"I don't want any interruptions when we get back to your place," was his simple response. "All right, we've got a monster turkey sub for me and a toasted chicken salad sub for the beautiful lady," he announced while peering into the large white-and-green checkered bag.

"I'm gonna miss all this when it's over," County lamented, resting against the cushioned backseat and watching Fernando extract the sandwiches.

His movements halted at her words and he slanted her a curious look.

"Being pampered," she clarified, watching the expression leave his handsome face.

"Are you expecting that?" he asked, setting aside the food in order to remove the black leather bomber jacket he wore.

County closed her eyes and sighed. "Things happen."

"Yes, they do," he agreed, tossing his coat to the opposite seat. "Things are definitely going to happen," he promised, facing her fully, "but that's not one of them."

In a split second, Contessa found herself scandalously entwined with his powerful form. Fernando's big hands cupped beneath her arms while he arched her into his kiss.

County moaned breathlessly. She was completely content allowing this man to bend her to his desire. His kiss demanded participation that she willingly obliged. Their tongues dueled slowly and with a shocking thoroughness that elevated their arousal to an even fierier pitch.

County tugged her bottom lip between her teeth to stifle her cries, soon to become screams of delight. Mouth trailing her neck, his hands roamed every inch of the mulberry cashmere cardigan shirt she wore with figure flattering black slacks. She writhed against him unashamed of the way he affected her. Fernando toyed with the buttons momentarily then made quick work of them. He broke the kiss when more of her body was exposed to his view.

Trailing her fingers through her glossy, boyish cut, Contessa chanted Fernando's name. Her nipples strained madly against the lace cups of her bra as though they were begging for release. Fernando seemed to hear their plea, but freed only one of the rigid buds, capturing it between his perfect teeth. He began to suckle just as a cell phone chimed in the distance.

"Damn," he growled, amidst the voracious feasting of his mouth against her bosom. Expressing clear reluctance to leave her, he pulled away slowly. "Don't you dare," he commanded, when County moved to fix her bra. "What?" he snapped into the receiver. His hypnotic gaze following the path his thumb trailed around one nipple.

County let her lengthy lashes flutter close and enjoyed the light, yet satisfying caress until it stopped.

Fernando's expression had hardened and he muttered a wicked expletive. "Are you sure?" he demanded to know.

Terence Newsome, one of the club's managers sighed before repeating his news. "The girls who left are working as hostesses on a ship called *The Wind Rage*."

"Doing what?"

"Well, Fern, it's a gentlemen-only ship, so…"

"Damn," Fernando could only whisper, bowing

his head to massage the bridge of his nose. *He was the proud owner of a sex ship. Yippee!*

"What you want me to do, man?" Terence asked.

"Nothing right now T, I'll be in touch and we'll meet before I leave for Seattle." Fernando decided. "Talk to you later." He clicked off the phone.

County had already fixed her clothes and sat watching him. "Everything okay?" she asked, not caring for the set look to his profile or the way his hand smoothed across the front of the blue-and-gray paisley print shirt he sported.

"Business," he explained after a silent minute.

"Wanna talk about it?" County asked, folding her legs beneath her.

"Not at all," he said.

There was no coldness in his voice, but County could tell whatever the *business,* it had him in an awful mood. "Why don't we postpone tonight so you can go handle it?" she encouraged.

Fernando's grin appeared, sparking the adorable crinkle of his eyes. "No way are you getting rid of me tonight, Ms. Warren."

"But you're obviously upset," County argued, though she loved the sound of his words. "You may not be in the mood for—"

"Yes, I am upset and being with you is the one thing that has a chance in hell of relaxing me."

County propped her elbow against the seat and rested her cheek next to her fist. "Why Mr.

Ramsey, you say the sweetest things," she said, pretending to gush.

Fernando was serious, however. "The words are easy to say when they're true," he said and pulled her snug into his lap.

The cool teasing in Contessa's brown eyes grew warm with passion. "Oh" was all she cold muster before he captured her parted lips in another explosive kiss. Eagerly, she suckled his tongue when it thrust savagely past her teeth. Her body was weak with desire, but she couldn't resist grinding herself onto the arousal rising beneath his navy trousers. When he cupped her hips to situate her in a more accommodating manner upon the stiff ridge of his manhood, County ordered herself to slow things down.

"No," he refused, when she tried to move.

"We should eat," she suggested.

"Later."

"Now," she decided, cupping his face in her palms, "I don't want any interruptions when we get to my place," she repeated his earlier words.

Fernando winked. "Good point," he said and effortlessly placed her back to her side of the car seat. "Now let's see," he said, returning his attention to the bag of food.

"Yes, I'll certainly miss this," County lamented, resting her head back against the seat, "for the next two weeks, anyway."

"Explain," Fernando urged, passing County her toasted chicken salad sandwich.

"Mick's shower party?" she clarified, "I'll be going to Seattle next Friday."

"Oh, yeah." Fernando grinned, adding extra tomatoes to his monster turkey sub. "She called and demanded my presence too," he remembered. "So why are you leaving so early? The party isn't until the end of the month."

County cut her sandwich in half. "We've really been missing each other. We just want some time together beforehand."

"So you can't make time for me during those two weeks?" he asked, biting down into the sandwich.

Contessa's brows rose, but she offered no response. Instead, she took a huge bite of the zesty sandwich. Munching filled the car for several moments. Fernando was halfway through his sub, when he noted that she had not uttered a reply.

Meanwhile, County went on eating and enjoying. It didn't take long however, to feel the beckoning translucent stare fixed her way. "What?" she questioned innocently.

"May I have an answer to my question?"

"Ramsey, I don't know how much time we'll have," she replied flippantly. "I mean, it's been a while since Mick and I really got together."

"That really it?" he asked, folding his arms across his chest and watching her try hard to swallow. "Spill it," he said. "Contessa," he called, when she stubbornly refused to talk.

"Dammit Ramsey, I don't want them to know about us, all right?!"

"Them? Who? Mick and Quest?"

"Your entire family."

"Why?"

County fixed him with a look that practically radiated the phrase *you're an idiot.* "Are you joking?" she said instead.

"Do you see me smiling?" Fernando challenged the brows above his deep-set gaze drawn close.

"Why? you ask," County repeated, bracing her elbows on her knees as she clasped her hands. "*Why,* because my House is working on a tell-all book about them. *Why,* because I don't want to have to deal with Mick and her questions. *Why* because your father is a jack—sorry. Let's just say he wouldn't take this well."

Fernando's caramel brown face was a picture of confusion. "Do you care? Because I don't," he confided, watching her hold her head in her hands. "Is this how you want us to be? Seeing each other in secret?"

"Listen, don't make me out to be the bad guy," County snapped, her lovely features taut with anger. "I'm willing to bet my ass you haven't told a soul in your family."

The confusion of Fernando's expression changed

to wicked intensity. "Is that a bet you're prepared to cash in?" he almost whispered.

County blinked. "You told someone?"

"Mmm-hmm," he confirmed with a simple nod, before reaching for the rest of his sub. Contentedly, he munched on the sandwich, knowing she was watching him in disbelief. "What?" he cried, when she slapped his shoulder.

"Who?"

"What?"

"*Who* did you tell?"

"Oh. My mother."

Stunned, County flopped back against the seat. "You told your mother about me?" she asked, disbelief flooding her words.

Fernando continued to devour his sandwich. "Of course I did."

"Do you tell her about all of your women?"

"Only in passing," he shared, around a mouthful of food. "I doubt I've ever mentioned one of them by name."

Quiet for a time, Contessa ate more of her sandwich and assessed what she'd learned. After polishing off chips and her sweet tea, she blurted, "What makes *me* so special, then?"

Fernando set aside his food, wiped his mouth and looked right into her eyes. "You're the *only* one I've ever fallen in love with."

Chapter 9

Contessa felt sick and it had nothing to do with the delicious deli meal she'd just enjoyed. Fernando was in love with her. He was in love with her and she was snooping around into his business. She was uncovering things that were potentially illegal and he was in love with her. She was in love with him. She was so very much in love with him too.

Fernando locked the front door to the condo and followed County inside. His expression was thoughtful as he removed his coat and gloves while watching her dazedly trying to do the same. When she fumbled over the top button of the trench, he went to assist.

"Did I scare you?" he asked, smothering her hands within his.

Contessa blinked. "Scare me? No— No Ramsey."

Fernando shrugged and unfastened the button. "Women have said it to me before and it scared the living hell out of me," he admitted.

"Did it scare you to say it?" County inquired softly, studying him through her thick lashes.

He curved a hand beneath her chin. "Not a bit," he swore.

"Fernando I—"

"Shh," he urged, giving her chin a squeeze. "I don't need you to reciprocate. I can wait."

The confidence masking his baritone voice brought a smile to her face. "You're so sure I'll fall in love with you, Ramsey?"

"You already have," he said, removing her leather trench and gloves. He grinned at the surprise on her lovely honey-toned face. Then, he nuzzled his nose against hers in an adoring gesture before he kissed her.

A helpless whimper escaped her mouth just as Fernando captured it fully with his own. She responded instantly and eagerly thrusting, caressing and stroking his tongue with the same leisurely desire he bestowed upon her. Contessa hardly noticed that in addition to helping her out of her coat, he'd quickly relieved her of the blouse and trousers she wore. He lifted her and she kicked off

KIMANI PRESS™

An Important Message from the Publisher

Dear Reader,

Because you've chosen to read one of our fine novels, I'd like to say "thank you"! And, as a special way to say thank you, I'm offering to send you two Kimani Romance™ novels and two surprise gifts – absolutely FREE! These books will keep it real with true-to-life African-American characters that turn up the heat and sizzle with passion.

Please enjoy the free books and gifts with our compliments...

Linda Gill

Publisher, Kimani Press

Peel off Seal and Place Inside...

THE EDITOR'S "THANK YOU" FREE GIFTS INCLUDE:

▸ Two NEW Kimani Romance™ Novels
▸ Two exciting surprise gifts

YES! I have placed my Editor's "Thank You" Free Gifts seal in the space provided at right. Please send me 2 FREE books, and my 2 FREE Mystery Gifts. I understand that I am under no obligation to purchase anything further, as explained on the back of this card.

PLACE
FREE GIFTS
SEAL
HERE

168 XDL ELWZ   368 XDL ELXZ

FIRST NAME   LAST NAME

ADDRESS

APT.#   CITY

STATE/PROV.   ZIP/POSTAL CODE

Thank You!

The Reader Service — Here's How It Works:

Accepting your 2 free books and 2 free gifts places you under no obligation to buy anything. You may keep the books and gifts and return the shipping statement marked "cancel." If you do not cancel, about a month later we'll send you 4 additional books and bill you just $4.69 each in the U.S. or $5.24 each in Canada, plus 25¢ shipping & handling per book and applicable taxes if any.* That's the complete price and — compared to cover prices of $5.99 each in the U.S. and $6.99 each in Canada — it's quite a bargain! You may cancel at any time, but if you choose to continue, every month we'll send you 4 more books, which you may either purchase at the discount price or return to us and cancel your subscription.

*Terms and prices subject to change without notice. Sales tax applicable in N.Y. Canadian residents will be charged applicable provincial taxes and GST. All orders subject to approval. Books received may vary. Credit or debit balances in a customer's account(s) may be offset by any other outstanding balance owed by or to the customer. Please allow 4 to 6 weeks for delivery.

If offer card is missing write to: The Reader Service, 3010 Walden Ave., P.O. Box 1867, Buffalo, NY 14240-1867

BUSINESS REPLY MAIL
FIRST-CLASS MAIL   PERMIT NO. 717-003   BUFFALO, NY

POSTAGE WILL BE PAID BY ADDRESSEE

THE READER SERVICE
3010 WALDEN AVE
PO BOX 1867
BUFFALO NY 14240-9952

NO POSTAGE
NECESSARY
IF MAILED
IN THE
UNITED STATES

the stylishly bulky black heels. She relished the friction of her body clothed only in peach silk tap pants, hose and a lacy bra as it rubbed against the fine material of his shirt and pants.

Fernando's intention was to take her to the bedroom. He could make it no farther than the stairway, where his powerful legs seemed to give out beneath him. Seated along the carpeted stairs, he straddled her across his lap and began to feast on her breasts.

Contessa buried her fingers in the silky crop of his brown curls, pressing his gorgeous face deeper into her chest. Fernando groaned, filling his palms with the ample mounds of cleavage. His teeth raked her nipple—half in, half out of her bra and already rigid with need. He suckled only for a moment and then favored the other with the same erotic torture. County ground herself over the steel length of his arousal—silently pleading for him to stop teasing her. At last, he obliged, removing the bra even as he caressed a pouting nipple with a hungry tongue.

County's fingers shook with desire as she unbuttoned his shirt and splayed her hands across the chiseled massive wall that was his chest. Her arousal intensified when the impressive pecs flexed in response to her touch. Her thumbnails brushed his nipples and she moaned when he drew her closer.

Still feasting on her breasts and the delicate skin beneath, Fernando sought to free himself from the confines of his trousers. He muttered a soft curse of approval when County tugged the zipper down and massaged his stiffness.

Fearing he was only a second away from release, Fernando made her stand and remove what remained of her undergarments. County smiled when he produced a condom from the back pocket of his trousers.

"Always prepared?" she noted.

"With you, I have to be," he said.

Again, his big hands cupped her hips to settle her across his huge frame. Contessa's breathless cry echoed in the silence of the space. Never, had she been so fulfilled by any man. Fernando's length was almost equally matched by his girth and he made expert use of both attributes. County's nails curved into the flawless caramel-toned skin of his shoulders, leaving half moon impressions. Fernando cupped the back of her head, massaging the silky hair where her cut tapered into a perfect V. His other hand squeezed her hips, urging her fully onto his iron power.

County tugged her bottom lip between her teeth as his invasion forced a wealth of moisture past the petals of her love. She smiled when Fernando uttered a surprised gasp in response to the subtle contractions she applied to his length.

"Stop," he groaned, squeezing her bottom in an attempt to control her movements.

She was full of wicked temptation. "Why?"

Fernando only groaned again, his impossibly long lashes fluttering as sensation overwhelmed him. His arousal lengthened and swelled even more each time he felt her walls tense purposefully around his manhood.

Reveling in her control over the massive god with the gentle touch, County assumed the lead. Slowly, she rode him: grinding ever so often, then easing off before he reached satisfaction. His hands were filled with her derriere, but he had no strength and rested his forehead against her shoulder. The foyer came alive with an ocean of deep male cries of pleasure. Soon, Contessa felt as powerless as Fernando. Her hips rocked and rotated as she sought to take all he had to give. At last, his grip tightened and he was thrusting up into her with shocking lunges that sent more moisture tumbling forth and sheathing his granite desire with her creamy need. Thoroughly weakened then, Contessa was merely a trembling mass. She held on to Fernando and increased the intensity of her ride, wanting to bring him to where she was. Fernando tried to resist, wanting the moment to last an eternity. County's skill triumphed however, and soon he was moaning his approval into the hollow of her throat. Their physical needs were satiated for a time, yet the arousal continued to pulse like a living throbbing thing just below the surface. They remained on the stairs for quite some time, clutched in a heated embrace.

* * *

"What?" Fernando probed later, as he massaged her foot, ankle and calf while she lounged on the bed.

County's smile was a mixture of laziness and curiosity. "I'd love to know how you made the transition from such a bad boy to a gentle masseur."

Fernando chuckled, instantly igniting the crinkles at the corners of his eyes. "That's a long, ugly story," he told her.

"With a happy ending," she said and flexed her toes until he looked at her. "So that would definitely make it worth hearing," she finished.

Fernando shook his head, his expression turning serious. "When I think about all the crap I used to pull…seems like it was a different guy."

"What made you do it?"

Again, Fernando shook his head and concentrated on her other foot. "I believe for a while I thought I was just trying to get attention because my dad was so *disinterested.* That was a cop-out."

A frown furrowed Contessa's soft brow. "Why would you think that? It's a perfectly understandable reason."

"I'd have done it anyway," he admitted, leaving her feet and coming to rest his head against her bare chest, "I had a lot of anger inside me, County. It needed a way out."

"Anger at who? Your father?" she guessed, stroking his hair where it lay at his temple.

"Anger at the way things were," he explained and clenched a fist near her hip. "Do you know lots of my best friends were guys who had no home, no food, barely had clothes on their backs? And there I was, bitchin' 'cause my dad worked too much?" he said, pounding his fist to the bed with light, repetitive motions. "Hell, it was *because* he worked so much that I had everything I wanted."

County pressed a kiss to his head. "A parent's time is all a kid really needs."

"A kid needs to eat, Contessa."

She nudged him with her shoulder. "You know what I mean."

Fernando grimaced. "It's hard to look at that when I saw my boys goin' to a shelter for dinner instead of their homes. Hmph, the ones who had homes were no better off," he recalled, propping his fist against the side of his face while resting his weight on his elbow. "I met a guy who became one of my best friends while me and Pop were spending a father and son day together." He grinned. "That was a laugh. My dad spent most of the day dragging me from one business meeting to another. We stopped by one of his apartment buildings. Another laugh," he said, his brown eyes darkening as they traced the outline his fingers made across County's stomach. "That building was barely standing. Nobody should have to live the way that guy and his mom did."

"Fernando," County soothed, hearing the pain color his voice when he spoke of his friend. She feathered his cheek with tiny kisses.

"That's when I first started to lose respect for my father. To let a kid and his mother live that way—at least my friend was almost grown. I remember seeing real little kids runnin' around half dressed, crying 'cause they were cold or a rat had just taken a nip at their toe." Fernando shook his head and relaxed on the bed again. "I grew real close to that guy," he said, thinking about Stefan Lyons then, "I was closer to him than my own brothers, I think. Pop even put him through school."

"Marcus?" County probed, surprised and impressed. "Very generous to help a wayward kid like that," she noted.

"I believe it was a genuine gesture," Fernando admitted with a chuckle. "I don't think my pop was always a conniving jackass. That time, I guess he just wanted to do a good thing," he shrugged. "Maybe he's acted so foul all these years because he was so used to everyone thinkin' the worst of him and he just didn't give a damn."

"Is that how *you* were?" County asked, resting on her elbow to look down at him.

"I guess," he admitted with a roll of his eyes.

County pressed her lips together and studied the striking breadth of his chest. She decided it would be the perfect time to tell him what was going on.

Fernando, however, had other ideas. Her breast nudged his fingers and soon they were fondling and squeezing the nipple until it had firmed.

"Wait," she whispered, her lashes already fluttering in response. "Fernando I have something to say."

"Later," he urged, moving to capture one nipple between his perfect teeth. His fingers fondled the other.

"Fernando…"

He rose, forcing her to lie back as he half covered her with his broad form. "Baby, I'm all talked out. Later? Please?" he whispered, his words growing faint as he buried his face between her breasts.

Contessa heard a low grumbling growl sound from the depths of his muscular torso and succumbed. "Ramsey," she tried again.

"Let it wait," he soothed.

Quest and Quaysar stood in a long hug. Their silent bond said more than any words could have. Clearly, they'd missed one another but Quest knew his twin had his reasons for staying away.

"So what now?" he asked when they'd stepped back from one another.

"Guess I'll try dealin' with Marcus," Quay sighed, massaging the tight muscles in his neck, "I know it'll be impossible to avoid it. Unless his ass is on the run too," he added, with a grim smirk.

"And you know that won't happen," Quest said, slapping his brother's shoulder as he stepped past.

"You're sure?"

Stopping midstride, Quest sent his brother a narrowed gray black look. "You're still on that?" he asked in disbelief.

Quay's expression was answer enough.

"You still think Marc's got somethin' to hide?" Quest persisted.

"Please don't tell me you think he's lily white?" Quay snapped.

"Hell no, but murder?"

"It was good enough for Houston."

"And tryin' to frame us for it?" Quest challenged. "Remember, it was Houston who always had a beef with Pop."

Quay rolled his eyes and headed toward the bar in his brother's den. "I don't know, Q. I guess I just want them fools out of this family so damn bad… before anymore crap turns up."

"You say Wake told you he was a cleanup man for this guy?"

"Right."

"And that the man he worked for hated dad with a passion?"

"Yeah and?"

"*And,* it just makes more sense for this to be about Houston than Marc," Quest decided, taking a seat on the sofa. "After all, it was Pop who took Ma off Houston's arm."

"Yeah," Quay slowly agreed, using his index

finger to stir the ice cubes in his glass of bourbon. "Something just doesn't fit, there's got to be more to it."

"Quay—why're you so worried about this?"

"Been on my mind since I've been away," Quay shared, turning to face his brother. "What if Houston isn't the only one with skeletons in his closet?"

"I think you're reaching," Quest said, crossing his jean clad legs as he rested his bare feet on the coffee table.

Quay's eyes narrowed almost to the point of closing. "Reaching?" he parroted.

"Hell, yeah, you just want someone to take out your anger on because you can't get your hands on Houston."

"Dammit Q, can you blame us! Hell, it's because of Houston that I lost all that time with Ty and that shit makes me mad enough to kill."

Quest folded his arms across his chest and studied his brother closely. He knew Quay's words were no idle threat. His temper was well earned and well feared. "Let it go Quay," he urged softly. "Focus on what you have now instead of what you lost back then."

Quest was right, as usual. Quay thought. "I just don't trust myself to see the man," he confided.

"I hope you're not just saying this to get out of coming to the party," Quest probed, his narrowing gray eyes twinkling with sudden humor.

Quay couldn't help but chuckle. "Mick won't have it, huh?"

"Not a chance in hell."

"You know Q, if *you* talked to her—"

"*Hell* no. I swear that girl's gotten stronger since she's been pregnant. One wrong word from me and she's liable to hit me hard enough to loosen some teeth," Quest predicted, joining his brother in hearty laughter. "Seriously though, man," he said when they sobered, "just take it easy. Marc knows how everyone feels about him. With any luck, he won't even show up."

"All right. Tomorrow? Sounds good," Fernando said as he arranged the meeting with one of the club's other managers. "Was there any other information?" he asked.

Contessa walked into the kitchen then, wearing a lavender T-shirt that scarcely covered her bottom. Fernando's attention was wholly focused on her as she went to study the contents of her cabinets. His call ended shortly and then he tossed aside the phone.

County smiled when she felt him behind her, massaging her hips before his hands curved around her thighs. He pulled her snug against his semi-hard arousal and for a time, they savored the embrace.

"Everything okay?" she asked after a while.

"Mmm-hmm," he murmured against her hair. "You hungry?"

"Starving," County admitted, nudging his chest with the back of her head, "that sandwich didn't hold out against our earlier activities."

"Well then," he said, squeezing her hips before setting her aside, "I should fix you something better. I don't want you giving out on me later."

"And what's later?" County teased, her vibrant browns widening when he turned to tower over her.

"You know what's later," the bass of his voice rumbled.

County's eyes lingered on his lips for a suggestively long time and soon after, she was crushed against Fernando's chest. His tongue thrust harshly inside her mouth and she groaned, loving the pressure.

Fernando frowned, knowing he had to let her go before his hormones got the better of him.

"Get away from me," he ordered, putting at least five feet of space between them.

County obeyed and chose a spot on one of the bar stools lining the counter. The easy look she wore seemed to fade after a while and she appeared serious. Deciding then, that the time for stalling was over, she began to speak, telling Fernando all she'd discovered.

As she spoke, his movements slowed. By the time she was done, he'd turned away from the stove and simply watched her. County cleared her throat, dragging her eyes away from the slow steady rise and fall of his bare chest. "You know, I *am* investigating your family for this book so I have every right to be looking into things like this," she rambled, not caring for the set look on his face.

Suddenly, Fernando smiled, easing his hands into the deep pockets of the sleep pants he'd taken to leaving at Contessa's house and which were presently slung low on his hips. "My guys are slow," he acknowledged softly, "I only got the call about the girls working on the ship while we were in the car."

"Wait, you—you didn't know?" County asked, blinking steadily.

Fernando shrugged. "I've known about the girls working on the ship for about four hours. It's why I'm meeting with my managers. I discovered I owned the ship a couple of days ago." He explained and turned back to the stove. "Why'd you tell me this?" he asked, selecting the temperature for the oven.

County propped her chin against her fist. "Because a woman shouldn't keep such things from the man she loves."

Silence held the kitchen captive for the longest time. At last, Fernando turned.

Contessa already knew what words waited on his breath. "I felt this way long before you told me," she admitted.

"Why didn't you say anything?" he asked in whisper.

"Pride wouldn't let me," she lowered her gaze to the counter. "I couldn't risk not hearing you say it back to me because at first I thought I was just floating on a cloud of lust and infatuation. Now, I believe it's more than that." She looked at him. "I feel I can go a little longer without my mask when I'm with you."

Fernando stroked the side of his beard. "A *little* longer? You feel you still need to wear it?"

"I've worn it so long," she sighed, "Mick's been the only one who could see the real me, but even then…"

"What?" he prodded, taking a stool next to her.

Raking all ten fingers through jet black locks, County grimaced. "I think I've let that mask slip into place around my dearest friend. Mick's got the wrong idea about me on so many things and honestly, Ramsey, I've done my best to give her those ideas. For so long I've told myself I don't want or need love. Physical satisfaction would do on occasion because I had more important things to contend with. Hmph, I guess I've even been wearing that mask for myself."

"We all do," Fernando said, nudging her shoulder with his own. "When there are things we can't admit to ourselves *about* ourselves."

County's fingers toyed with his while she marveled at the manner in which his hand practically engulfed her own. "I only know that I wanted to be honest with you. I want you to know everything about me and that's dangerous."

"Why dangerous?"

"The people who know the most about you can hurt you the most because they have more to hurt you with."

Fernando watched as she lowered her eyes to shield the pain he knew dwelled there. "You believe I'd hurt you?"

"I don't know and in spite of that I still can't pull away from you," she squeezed his hand. "*That* scares me."

Fernando pressed a kiss to the top of her head. This time, it was his turn to debate. It didn't take him long to decide that the time had come for him to tell her he was part owner in the company trying to take Contessa House. He was opening his mouth to voice the confession when the sound of his cell phone pierced the air.

County amused herself tracing the patterns imbedded within the countertop. She froze when she heard him whisper— "What?" into the phone. With effort, he managed to thank the person on the line and then end the call. She waited, wondering if he'd tell her. She didn't have long to wait.

"Houston's in jail," he said.

Chapter 10

Michaela's plump, dark brown face glowed more than usual as she watched the limo rounding the horseshoe drive. She screamed when County finally emerged from the back of the car sent to fetch her from the airport courtesy of Ramsey Group. The two met on the steps of the massive front porch and hugged for the longest time. They stood talking about everything and nothing—trying to catch up in the span of ten seconds.

"This tummy of yours," County sighed when they pulled out of another hug. "Are you sure there're no twins in there?"

"Hush," Mick chastised, smacking Contessa's

shoulder, "and what's going on with you? I thought only us pregnant ladies glowed like that."

"What?" County asked, her voice still colored by laughter.

"You look beautiful."

County shrugged. "I always look beautiful."

Mick rolled her eyes. "Well, this time someone other than *you* can see it," she jibed, shrieking playfully when County tugged on one of her curls. "Seriously though, you look radiant—even if you're not smiling."

"I guess the plane ride was surprisingly good. Not to mention riding in luxury from the airport," County excused with a flip wave.

Mick folded her arms such that they rested atop her belly. "It's more than that…who is he?"

"Jeez Mick, just 'cause you're all goo-goo over love doesn't mean the rest of us are," County blurted, averting her gaze to hide her nerves.

Mick was far from convinced. "I guess I'll just have to wait until you're ready to share."

"Anyway," County groaned, finding a place to slip her sunglasses into her bag, "so tell me about Houston," she asked, desperate for a subject change.

"Girl, it's been all the talk," Mick said, easing both hands into the pockets of her pink linen capris.

"Details?"

"It's strange," Mick admitted, her amber gaze narrowing suddenly, "he eluded capture all those months and then gets himself picked up at a restaurant. He was just sitting out in the clear blue like everything's everything."

County fidgeted with the tassels on her long-sleeve white cotton top. "Has he said anything?" she asked.

"More strangeness. He keeps saying he won't go down alone and that he was set up."

County laughed. "It's a little late to use that!"

"I'll say," Mick drawled, a tiny frown furrowing her brow. "Anyway, how'd *you* find out so fast? It just happened."

"You underestimate how important that piece of news is even all the way out in Chicago," County said, slapping one hand to the stylishly short pleated navy skirt she sported. "Besides, I'm still investigating the family, remember?"

"So have you found another author to take over the book?" Mick asked, trying to downplay her intense interest.

"We're still gathering facts *and* looking for an author," County informed, slanting her best friend a sly look. "I gotta make sure I choose the right person and someone I can count on not to fall in love with one of the beautiful Ramseys."

"Well, that should be you, then," Mick said in a amused tone. "You've been around them almost as much as I have and still you've managed not to fall under their spell."

Contessa cleared her throat, failing to prevent the unsettled look from returning to her face.

"Dammit County, what the hell is going on?" Mick demanded, easily spotting her friend's unease.

County threw up her hands. "I really wish you'd stop asking me that," she hissed, brushing past Mick to head into the house.

"There she is!" Quest bellowed as he arrived in the foyer. His soft laughter filled the space when he and County shared a hug.

"So tell me about this party?" County asked when she and Quest pulled apart.

Mick was instantly focused on her get-together. "I'm expecting a very nice crowd next weekend," she predicted, clasping her hands to her chest. "The first night will be the fruit cocktail party," she shared, her amber stare excitement-filled.

County and Quest exchanged glances.

Mick was undaunted. "If I can't have a real cocktail, then no one else will."

"This is *your* best friend." Quest told County.

She patted her hand against the front of his Seahawks T-shirt. "This is your wife *and* baby's mama," she retorted.

Quest's long lashes closed over his gray-black stare. "Help me Lord," he prayed.

"Dr. Harris White for Houston Ramsey."

The two security guards scrutinized the tall, thin man who arrived at their station.

"He ain't sick, buddy," one of the guards informed Dr. White.

"Oh, he's sick all right," the other guard said with a sly grin, "sick his rich ass got caught."

"I'm Mr. Ramsey's psychiatrist," the doctor explained once the chuckling guards quieted. "I've been appointed by the family," he went on, placing official-looking papers on the desk before the two men.

"What's he need with a psychiatrist?"

Dr. White lost what little patience he had and snatched up the papers. "I'll be happy to have you both served if you continue to hinder me from visiting my patient."

"Sorry doc," one of the guards said as he sobered beneath the man's steely glare.

"Right this way," guard number two instructed, holding open a door and waving Harris White toward the visitors area.

"Houston Ramsey is under my care and I'll need privacy to administer treatment," the doctor said upon seeing the semicrowded visiting area.

The guards exchanged glances. Their patience for the haughty doctor had grown thin as well.

"I'll be happy to speak with your supervisors on this matter," Harris White threatened subtly.

Making silent decisions to give the man what he wanted to accelerate his departure, the guards obliged. They had him wait in a spacious quiet room with cement walls. The light blue paint, two way mirror and long chrome table were the only adornments.

Houston arrived looking hopeful. A frown soon emerged on his face when he spotted the stranger in the room.

"Dr. Harris White."

"Doctor?" Houston inquired, his frown deepening as he studied the blandly dressed man.

"Psychiatrist," Dr. White clarified.

Houston's anger went from simmer to boil in the span of ten seconds. "I don't need a shrink!" he snapped, pounding his fist to his palm. "What the hell is this?!"

"Easy Houston."

"Don't call me Houston. You don't know me! Who sent you? They're tryin' to shut me up, aren't they?"

"Mr. Ramsey—"

"Aren't they? Well I'm sick of hiding the truth and looking like the devil of the family!"

"Houston, you're overreacting," Dr. White acknowledged in a manner that was frightfully calm. "You need something to relax you," he explained while strolling closer.

Before Houston could react, Dr. White had closed the distance between them and injected a needle into his arm.

"What—what'd you give me?" Houston barely had time to ask before he stumbled and slumped against the table.

The doctor caught Houston's chin and tilted his head back to peer into his eyes. Nodding with satisfaction, he replaced the hypodermic needle inside his beige suit coat pocket.

"I'll be back tomorrow," he promised his woozy patient before turning for the door. "Guard!" he called.

Fernando was in a foul mood by the end of the meeting with his managers. The group had no more evidence on what the girls were doing aboard *The Wind Rage, owned and operated, by yours truly,* he drily noted. His managers wanted to know when he'd be heading back to Seattle, nodding solemnly when he told them within a couple of hours. They realized how difficult the situation was with his family—his uncle Houston more specifically. Fernando could only hope the drama was nearing its end. He thanked the group for their concern, and then waited until they'd exited his office before making his call.

"Hey Mr. J," he greeted in a tone that was both hearty and humble. "This is Fernando Ramsey."

Jeff Carnes's chuckle came as a low rumble when he recognized the name. "This is quite a surprise, young man. How've you been?"

"Pretty good," Fernando said, reclining in his desk chair and fanning his cobalt polo tee away from his chest.

"Mmm…now tell me the truth."

"Damn Mr. J. How do you do that?" Fernando marveled, his brown eyes narrowed in wonder.

"I'm a lawyer. More importantly I'm a father and that alone gives me a wealth of insight. Now talk," the man ordered.

"It's about my father."

"I see."

"Actually it's about his boat. *The Wind Rage.* You're his lawyer and I hoped you could tell me a little about it."

"The Wind Rage…" Jeff sighed, his cheerful voice dropping an octave as a tightness set in. "I haven't heard that name in a long time."

"But you *have* heard it?"

"Oh. yes."

Fernando sat straight. "Mr. J, I know you work for my dad—"

"No son. Not for many years."

"Not for many years?" Fernando parroted, stunned amazement filling his voice. "Pop never mentioned it."

"I'm sure he didn't," Jeff confirmed with a humorless grunt. "I quit shortly after our disagreement."

"Do you mind my asking about that disagreement?"

"Not at all. It was over that damned boat or maybe over the fact that he wanted to put it in your name."

Fernando massaged his eyes. "I just found out about it."

Jeff was momentarily speechless. "I can't believe Marc even told you," he marveled, tugging at the tie that was growing tight around his neck.

"He didn't. I discovered it on my own, so to speak."

"What's going on here Fernando?" Jeff asked, his intuition peaked.

"Mr. Carnes, you have to know what's happening with the family?"

"Hell, son, it's impossible to live in Seattle and *not* know."

"My father tried to help Houston cover up what he did. He succeeded for many years."

"I guess all this has you wondering what else your father is capable of?" Jeff asked.

"I want him gone, Mr. Carnes," Fernando spoke without hesitation, "I want him gone legally and if that ship is what I think it is, then I may be able to do just that."

"What do you think is going on?"

"Gambling, prostitution maybe."

"Mmm…"

"Mr. J? Can you confirm any of this? Will you?"

"Boy, are you sure you want to get into this?"

Fernando stroked his beard and grimaced. "I know too much to stop being curious about the entire story."

"I understand how you feel Fern, but sometimes

it's best to remain ignorant about all the ugly details," Jeff cautioned.

"But if I want peace in my family, Mr. J, then I'm afraid I need to hear every ugly detail."

Jeff's heavy sigh carried over the line for more than a few seconds. "All right Fernando," he conceded, "all right."

"Maybe you'll tell me about him if we go *out* for dinner."

"Will you please let it go?" County insisted, rolling her eyes toward her best friend.

"Just confirm that I'm right," Mick pleaded, pulling a pillow before her as she kneeled in the center of the queen-sized bed. "Come on, there *is* someone," she prodded.

"Mick…"

"Oh, come on County, that's the least you can do after the way you hounded me about Quest."

"That was different," County replied, idly focusing more on unpacking her clothes. "You and Quest had a future. Anyone could see that."

"So may I take that as a yes?"

Confused at first, Contessa turned to fix Mick with a frown. Then, she rolled her eyes and nodded. "Yes, there is someone," she admitted finally.

Mick's squeal pierced the room. "Details, details. Come on, spill it!"

"You said you only wanted confirmation."

Mick waved her hands about her head. "Reporters lie, you know that."

County turned back to her unpacking. "You ain't a reporter no more, Miss Mama-To-Be."

"That's right," Mick agreed with a finger poised in the air. "I'm a mama-to-be and now nosiness is in my blood. So how'd you two meet?"

"He's the reason I left before the balloons fell at James Aston's New Year's party."

"Oooooh! Ooooh! You scandalous hussy!" Mick bellowed, her amber gaze wide as she covered her mouth and wriggled on the bed.

County stiffened, her expression growing somber as her head bowed.

"I'm sorry County," Mick apologized, realizing that her friend's new relationship had a lot to do with her sensitive mood. "Honey, is everything okay?" she asked, uncertain if she should question.

Contessa left the closet, and then joined Mick on the bed. "It's just so complicated."

Mick bit her lip, fidgeting with the decorative edges of the hunter green and silver pillowcase as she debated. "Is he married?" she asked finally.

"Mick!"

"I'm sorry, I'm sorry. That's usually what *complicated* means," she explained quickly.

County raked her fingers through her cropped cut before smoothing both hands across her skirt. "No Mick, he's very much unattached."

"Well, then, what's the problem?" Mick demanded, her concerns clearly evident in her expression.

"He's wonderful," County admitted, her face aglow as Fernando Ramsey came to her mind. "He's beyond wonderful. He's gorgeous and attentive and sexy and big—"

"Big. Big as in…"

"Big. In every way."

Mick reclined on her bed, keeping the pillow in front of her stomach. "I thought you hated really big men—too overpowering."

Contessa smiled with a shrug. "I guess I've had a change of heart. The man's incredible and he treats me like Heaven."

"Then what's the problem?"

"Ah, Mick, where do I begin?" County sighed, flopping back on the bed. "There're just so many obstacles. For starters, I've got my suspicions about certain aspects of his business."

Mick rested her head on the pillow. "Illegal suspicions?" she probed.

"Mmm. Then, there's his family and before you say it—" she started upon seeing Mick's mouth open. "This is completely different from what you and Quest went through. His father is nothing like Damon."

"But *you're* Contessa Warren," Mick boasted, nudging County's side with her big toe.

"That's right and my life is just fine without all that drama."

"But you're in love."

County's smile froze. "I didn't pick up on it nearly that fast."

"It's a mama-to-be-thing." Mick shrugged. "Besides, I've never seen you look so radiant or talk this way before. You're clearly in love with this man."

Grunting tiredly, County left the bed and returned to unpacking.

"So who is he?" Mick asked after watching County rifle through her suitcase for close to a minute.

"Why?" County snapped and then cleared her throat.

"Don't you dare stand there and act like you're not gonna tell me who he is," Mick chastised, propping her elbow on the pillow. "At least tell me if I know him," she bartered.

County shook her head. "You know him," she confirmed.

"Thanks," Michaela chirped and relaxed upon the bed again, "now all I have to do is go through all the men we know in Chicago."

"All right," County smiled, not bothering to tell her friend that she wasn't even in the correct area code.

"What's goin' on, man?" Quest bellowed, pleased to find his first cousin on his front doorstep. He and Fernando shared handshakes and hugs, and then it was inside for drinks in the den.

"Did I interrupt anything?" Fernando asked after they'd chatted idly for a few moments.

A sly smile tilted the corners of Quest's mouth. "Unfortunately not," he shared, knowing what his cousin was asking. "County just got in so she and Michaela will probably go out and then be up all night talkin'."

"Contessa's here?" Fernando asked, his eyes narrowing to brown, deep-set slits.

"Yeah she—Fern?" Quest called, fixing his cousin with an uncertain stare. "Don't tell me?" he inquired softly, grinning at the look Fernando sent him. "Damn," Quest drawled thoroughly shocked as he folded his arms across the front of his North Carolina A&T sweatshirt. "Why the hell haven't you told anybody?" he went on to ask.

Fernando stroked his beard and went to refreshen his gin. "She wants to keep it quiet…for obvious reasons. I did tell Ma, though."

"I know she still has plans for a book on the family," Quest noted, stroking the fine hair at his temple, "how do you feel about that?"

"I don't give a damn about that book. I only want her."

Quest nodded, impressed yet surprised, in spite of the fact that he'd virtually fell in love with Michaela Sellars the first time he saw her. "I gotta admit it, man. I never thought you'd fall like this."

Fernando set his drink down and rolled up the

sleeves of the maple shirt he wore, "I don't know, Q. She's done somethin' to me and you may think I'm full of crap for saying this, but it goes *way* deeper than sexual."

Quest nodded, his gray-black gaze sparkling with understanding. "So is Dark Squires still interested in her publishing house? I recall your saying something about it a while back."

"I talked about it with Stef," Fernando said, the easiness in his face fading just a little, "I convinced him to drop it."

Quest's sleek brows rose. "I can't believe he didn't put up more of a fight. Your partner's a damn maniac when it comes to adding on to that company," he noted.

"Well it wasn't easy," Fernando admitted, taking his drink and strolling back to the armchair he'd occupied. "I think we're on the same page, though."

"Have you told her you own part of the company?"

Fernando buried his face in his hands. "Q, man," he groaned, his deep voice effectively muffled. "I tried, but the time is never right."

"And it's not something you're looking forward to?" Quest finished.

Fernando looked up. "Bingo."

"Tell her now, man," Quest warned, even though he sympathized with his cousin's reluctance, "it's all too easy for something like that to come out."

"You're right. You're right, but I'll have to handle it when I come back." Fernando explained, downing a bit of his drink.

"Back?" Quest inquired.

"Let's just say Uncle Houston's about to have some company in jail."

"Can't we just drive around and stop somewhere?" County asked, massaging her eyes.

Mick grimaced. "Not if we want something good. Besides we need to call and get a table so we can eat right after the show." She patted her belly through the pastel blue tee she wore. "You got a pregnant lady here, remember?"

"Well, girl, this is *your* town. Tell me something."

"Just keep checking the D's," Mick instructed hastily. "Darens, *Darons,* I can't remember the name of that place where me and Ty had dinner a few weeks ago."

"Well, I'm not having any luck here," County complained and expressed a weary smile.

Mick tilted her head. "You've got the white pages, lemme see if I can go find a yellow book. I've been tryin' to get Ty on the phone, but I can't get through on her cell or at home. Probably laid up in bed with Quay—the freaks," she muttered.

County grinned, but didn't look away from the phone book. "And look who's talkin' Miss Can't Stay Away From Quest Ramsey For An Hour."

Michaela shushed her friend, then left the room to hunt down the yellow pages. Contessa browsed absently, until her search through the D's turned up something unexpected. Listed clear as day between Darjels Nails and Braids and Dark and Tantalizing Gentleman's Club was Dark Squires Communications. *They're right here in Seattle—the bastards,* County thought, drily replaying her conversation with Stefan Lyons.

"Well, well, this trip won't end without a visit to *that* office," she vowed and reached for her book to jot down the number and address.

Chapter 11

"Are you sure?"

Fernando's gaze was solemn as he nodded toward his cousin. "Positive. Jeff Carnes confirmed…everything."

"And *he's* sure? I mean, is this secondhand info or—"

"He saw it with his own eyes, Quest. He saw it."

Quest smoothed both hands across the close cropped waves of his hair before standing from the chair he'd been glued to for the past twenty minutes. Once he and his cousin finished chatting about love and women, Fernando got to the point of his visit. It went without saying that he'd shocked his cousin to his soul.

"Have you told anyone?"

"Not even the managers at The Spot and this will affect them too."

"True," Quest agreed, massaging the brand in his left arm where the familiar ache had formed, "but it won't affect them near as much as it will the rest of the family. Does Aunt Josie know?" he asked, referring to Fernando's mother.

"I don't think so."

"But you can't be sure?"

"I've been more observant of her lately," Fernando said, brushing the back of his hand across his beard as he looked out over the back lawn, "I'd never really noticed the fear always in her eyes."

"So what do you think?" Quest asked after several moments of silence.

Fernando shrugged. "I don't know what to think, but Ma's a strong lady. She doesn't act on impulse and can bide her time better than anyone I know. I think she always suspected Marc of being truly evil, but had no proof. I think she would've used it if she had."

Quest nodded. "So what now?" he asked.

"I booked a spot on the next voyage."

"That safe, Fern?" Quest whispered, coming to stand next to his cousin. "Someone might recognize you, you know?"

Fernando shook his head. "I'm willing to chance it. Jeff Carnes says Pops is very serious about keeping what's goin' on with the ship a secret—his partners don't know what we look like."

"I don't know Fern. Hell, we're always in the news for some charity thing or business deal. Can you be sure no one knows you?"

"Look at what he's done to this family, Q," Fernando snapped, shoving his hands in his black trouser pockets while storming away from the den's sliding glass doors. "Houston?" he mentioned, slanting Quest a fierce look. "The man's sick and instead of getting him help, he covers for him, gets a medical examiner to hide evidence. All that time Quay and Ty wasted out of fear, what happened with Yohan and Melina, hell he almost ruined you and Mick before you got started and then my mother... it's got to end, man." He swore, waving his index finger in warning.

"But this is your life, Fern," Quest continued to reason. "If someone recognizes you on that ship, you could be killed. You willin' to risk that?"

"Most definitely." Fernando responded without a second's hesitation.

The stench was still there, clinging after all those years, Josephine would swear it. Oh sure, whenever Marc shared the bed, the sheets were in the garbage the next day—something no one knew but herself. Still, the stench was there—perhaps in her mind. *Now* in her mind. But once, it had been all too real.

How many nights, how many days had she come in from taking the boys to school, the playground, church…to discover him laid up in bed with two sometimes three women. The fact that she knew seemed to arouse him more. Still, she did nothing. She continued to wear the mask, to carry out the facade and play the role of the lovely graceful Josephine Simon Ramsey.

She told herself it was for the boys, but the boys would have been fine. It was her. It went without saying that Marc held all the cards. He'd easily worm his way out of alimony, she'd feared back then. She'd have to get a job and then…oh, that would be too much. To go from the heights of society grandeur to cleaning toilets for one of the families who envied the power behind the name she wore. No, she would wait. It would all come to pass. The affairs, the outside children, the crimes…she would have her time and…she did. She had quite a few times.

The money she so desperately wanted to hold on to had afforded her more than a fine house, it had afforded her pleasure, such sweet pleasure. Crane Cannon entered her life and she indulged over and over again—reaping the most delicious desire, the most satiating revenge.

Marc strutted so proudly over his beautiful son. Josephine floated over the spectacle he never realized he made of himself—taking such pride in a child that wasn't even his own.

Now Houston was behind bars and it looked as though Marc had turned his back on him—else he never would have been caught. Unfortunately, she couldn't sit and wait for her brother-in-law to act accordingly. Houston wasn't strong enough to bring Marc down with him. She'd been sure giving Sera's diary to Mick would've rattled Houston enough to tell all, but it hadn't; not even when the police were carting him off to jail. No. It would take more and although she swore to never seek that help, time was running out. She feared her husband would once again escape what he so richly deserved.

"I could eat a ton," Contessa groaned as she and Mick made their way downstairs.

"Ain't the truth," Mick concurred fluffing her curls, "we're gonna shut the place down."

County sent her friend a sly look. "With you for my dinner partner, I don't doubt it," she said and flinched when Mick swatted at her head.

The two were still teasing each other viciously when they heard male voices rising from the downstairs den. Quietly, they strolled to the doorway and Mick laughed when she saw Fernando. County hung back, watching her friend become enveloped in the man's bear hug.

"Sweetie lemme introduce you," Mick said, as she patted Fernando's chest, "County?" she called, waving her friend from the doorway. "You remember

Quest's cousin? Fernando Ramsey, my best friend and publisher Contessa Warren." Mick made the introductions, never noticing the emotion-filled looks passing between the two.

After a second or so, County could barely maintain eye contact with Fernando. She focused instead on his hand still holding her own. His fingers grazed her wrist with the slightest touch.

Mick had already moved on to tell her husband they were leaving and the moment between them grew heated as always. Quest was never bashful about kissing his wife senseless.

Of course, the steamy scene on the other side of the room only made things more difficult for Fernando and Contessa. She felt him tug on her hand. Her rich brown stare clashed with his translucent one and she quickly shook her head. Fernando's expression sharpened with agitation.

Thankfully, Quest and Mick's passionate kiss came to an end and she was turning to fetch her friend. Her lips parted in tell-tale fashion when she noticed Fernando still clutching Contessa's hand. She made no mention of it and simply asked County if she was ready and then told the guys they'd see them later.

Alone with his cousin, Quest walked over and clapped Fernando's shoulder.

Contessa was unusually silent on the way to the car. It had already been decided that she would be driving with Mick delivering directions. Mick waited until they were both seated inside her Infiniti SUV before she said a word.

"When you said he was big, you weren't just kidding."

Contessa had been setting her seat belt in place when she heard Mick's comment. She frowned, watching as her friend calmly checked her makeup.

Finally, Mick turned with a sweet smile on her face. "Excellent choice," she commended, with a saucy wink.

"Don't grill me over this please," County begged.

"I have no intention of doing that," Mick swore, raising her hand to testify, "but why are you so on edge about it? Fernando's great. Physically…magnificent and magnificent in other ways that I'm sure you're more than aware of."

"It's not that simple Mick," County argued, propping her elbow on the armrest and raking fingers through her short cut. "Fernando has a past that I fear is still very much a part of his future."

"Well, I know he's had some dealings with some rough people," Mick shared, folding her arms over the long-sleeved empire waist blouse she wore, "but all that other stuff he let go of years ago."

"You can't be sure of that."

"Well, dammit County, what the hell does it matter if you're in love with him?"

"Oh, hell, Mick!" County blurted with heavy

laughter. "Your head is still in the clouds about love. I guess that's as it should be, but Fernando is nothing like Quest."

"Really?" Mick challenged, turning to face her friend across the gear console. "He's sweet, kind, fiercely loyal and protective of his family—especially his mother and Yohan. But he's also very misunderstood. People look at him, think about his wild days and they're ready to condemn, throw it up in his face, making him relive it and never allowing him to escape it."

County trailed her fingers across the scoop neckline of her gray top. "Do you think he *wants* to escape it?"

"Yes, Count. Yes, I do. But it doesn't matter what I think, does it?"

County blinked to keep the sudden rush of tears from wetting her lashes. It didn't work. "I don't want to get hurt Mick."

"Said every woman who ever gave a man her heart," Mick sang, leaning over to kiss her friend's cheek. "I know you won't walk away from him, though. Complications and all. He's the first man that you're praying to keep in your life for the unforeseeable future."

"You're right," County admitted with a slow nod. "But I know they're still so many rocks in our path."

"Well, news flash, it's all right to be scared," Mick soothed, patting her hand. "But tell him this, stop hiding the fact that you're together 'cause you're both terrible at pretending." She said and nudged County's jean clad thigh as they laughed. "Now move it, I'm starving and in about ten minutes I'm gonna have to go the bathroom."

"How many more injections will he need?" Marcus asked, leaning back in the desk chair at his home office as he waited for a response on the other end of the line.

"Only two more," Dr. Harris White shared. "The man is already pretty unstable and with the medicine affecting his lucidity, his rambling will sound even more crazed. Now, tell me about this DNA test."

"Houston will submit to the test based on the advice of his lawyer." Marc assured the man.

Harris White grinned. "Of course he will, especially since *you're* retaining that lawyer. We're playing a deadly game here Marc," he cautioned upon sobering from a round of chuckles, "what Houston knows could ruin us all."

"That's only if anyone believes him and you're taking care of that," Marc said.

"I'm drugging him," Harris clarified. "It's up to you to make sure he's convicted and put away 'til we're all dead and buried. He's your brother and—"

"He's screwing with our business," Marc interrupted, no trace of sympathy touching his voice. "Don't worry about my brother. He's on his way out."

* * *

"Dammit," Josephine cursed where she waited outside Marc's office door. With Houston gone and Wake who knows where, her husband would never be punished for his sinister deeds. She had no choice but to make that call. She would have to say, do whatever it took, to get Melina back to Seattle.

Contessa took a deep, satisfying breath of late night Seattle air and smiled. She and Mick had a great time that night despite the fact that once she got there, thoughts of Fernando almost ruined her appetite. She couldn't get him off her mind. Luckily, her best friend's incessant rambling on everything from backache to creative sexual positions for accommodating her growing tummy, kept County's spirits high. Soon, she and Mick were pigging out with the best of them. The evening was great, but now, back in her bedroom at Quest and Mick's, her thoughts were again focused on Fernando Ramsey.

Mick was right. So what if Fernando had a dark past and elements of that past were still a part of his present? She wanted—loved—him and he said he felt the same.

Oh, where was that carefree girl from New Year's Eve? *Just enjoy this County and don't let all that other mess creep in,* she told herself. Sighing contentedly, she rested her head next to one of the French doors leading out to her balcony. After five seconds, she turned and wasn't surprised to find Fernando leaning against her doorway.

"What are you doing here?" she still asked, waving him inside.

Fernando shut the door. "It was open."

"No, it wasn't."

"Unlocked."

"Completely different."

"You're right."

More on edge now, County rubbed her hands across the capped sleeves of the peach T-shirt she wore with matching boy shorts. "What are you doing here?" she asked again.

"Contessa…" Fernando's drawl clearly answered the question.

County shivered and rolled her eyes. "What are you *still* doing here?" she rephrased.

Fernando nodded, deciding to be serious. "Quest and I kept talking after you left with Mick. We put a serious dent in his liquor stash and I didn't think it'd be a good idea to get behind the wheel."

"Very conscientious."

"Not really," he admitted, the eye-crinkling grin appearing. "I had ulterior motives."

County propped her hands on her hips. "Nooo," she sighed.

Strolling slowly, Fernando stalked until the distance closed between them. A lone finger extended to outline her breasts thrust so prominently against the snug tee.

"Ramsey…" County warned, even as her lashes fluttered in response to the sensation.

"Are you resisting me?" Fernando asked, crowding her space with his massive frame.

"We're not alone."

Fernando's laughter filled the room. "Love, anyone who spends a night with Quest and Mick knows they always put guests on the other side of the house unless there's some big soirée. I can pretty much guarantee they're already…busy."

"And you came here to follow in their footsteps?"

"Ah County, you wound me," he murmured, his lips feathering her brow, temple, the curve of her cheek. "I thought what we did tested new boundaries."

County felt her nipples grow rigid against his chest. "I'm flattered," she breathed.

"I'd much prefer you agree."

"Do you ever stop?" she laughed.

His hand curved around her neck. "Not until I get what I came for."

"Me?"

"Mmm…"

Words were pretty much irrelevant then. Fernando's head dipped and his lips came down on County's in an erotic wave of emotion. Her cries were muffled in her throat as his tongue thrust deep, hot, relentlessly and he left no part of her mouth unexplored. She tried to be an eager participant in the kiss, but found that she much preferred Fernando's suckling her tongue, outlining her lips and caressing the roof of her mouth.

Her ample bottom more than filled his big hands. Fernando felt his arousal swell a bit more in an instant reaction. Placing her on the oak dresser, he worshipped her shapely legs and thighs with wet, openmouthed kisses and leisurely strokes from his tongue. County tugged her bottom lip between her teeth in an effort to smother her moans. He pushed her thighs farther apart, bringing his mouth to the extrasensitive junction he discovered. County jerked in response to his lips and teeth nipping and his hair roughened face grazing the satiny skin he found there. When his tongue thrust fiercely against the middle of her shorts, she arched closer for more of the torturous caress. His mock feasting on her womanhood was almost as satisfying as the real thing, County decided, feeling her own moisture soak her clothing. She was aching to arch her breasts into his hands when his fingers squeezed and rubbed the nipples still hidden beneath her top.

An impatient grunt rumbled within Fernando's chiseled chest and soon he was pulling Contessa from the dresser and placing her on the floor. She treated herself to a moment of feeling helpless and at his mercy while looking up at him from her spot on the luxurious black carpeting. Her fingers trailed the length of her body, disappearing inside the crotch of her shorts as she watched him undress. She cried out when she touched the velvety folds of her sex. His shirt cast aside, Fernando felt a stab of jealousy when he saw where her fingers were. Going to his knees, he pushed them aside, and then set about stripping the clothing from her body. He held her wrists on either side of her head while his teeth grazed her nipples. A devilish smile curved his mouth when her helpless gasps filled his ears.

"Please," County sobbed, her toes insinuating themselves at the front of his trousers. Feeling the indescribable power straining near his zipper sent more moisture flooding onto her thighs.

Fernando left her breasts, traveling the length of her body until his nose caressed the bikini waxed, satiny smooth skin above her womanhood.

"Did I make you do this?" he teased, noticing the white cream upon her honey-toned thighs.

County was so weakened by desire she could only smile in response.

Fernando curved his hands beneath her bottom and began to dine on what he craved. He gave her a warning squeeze when she instinctively thrust against him. County splayed her fingers upon the carpet and tried to obey his silent request. Unashamed, she let loose her cries when his tongue ventured just slightly past the silky petals of her love.

He remained there for a while, lightly exploring, nibbling the bud of flesh he hungered for.

"Please…oh, please," County urged, needing to feel him fill her there. She bucked against his mouth when his tongue lunged deep, past the quivering flesh, inside her tight walls. County's cries mingled with Fernando's gravely moans. He seemed as affected as she, his tongue thrusting rapaciously as though he were determined to brand her with his mark. County felt his grip ease on her bottom and she began to thrust again, almost fainting from the increased sensation it provided. She was seconds away from climax when he stopped.

"Damn you," she hissed, slamming a fist against the brick wall of his chest.

Fernando grinned, effortlessly lifting her from the floor to place her on her stomach in the center of the bed. County felt limp as a wilted flower, burying her face in a pillow when her moans showed no signs of growing silent.

His translucent brown stare caressed her sensational form—which he found impossibly sensational from behind. Pulling a condom from his pocket, he unzipped his trousers and let the rest of his clothing fall away. County felt his hands grip her waist and she arched back against him. With protection in place, Fernando impaled her onto his magnificent length. His fingers reached around to fondle her even as he took her from behind. One hand cupped her breasts and kept her in place to take every bit of what he wanted to give her. County chanted his name each time she ground herself against him. Fernando gnawed her shoulder, manipulating her nipple the same way he manipulated the sensitized bud of flesh at her womanhood. All the while his savage thrusts forced her to produce floods of creamy moisture that drenched his manhood and welcomed him even deeper inside her body.

Chapter 12

Not surprisingly, Contessa dreamed of only one man and all the delicious things he'd done to her the night before. She woke with a groan of pleasure the following morning. Her fingers splayed out across the bed in search of Fernando, but only touched cold sheets where he'd rested just hours earlier. She was disappointed and at the same time thankful that he'd gone before Michaela came knocking. Having her find the two of them cuddled in bed together would be too much for Contessa to take from her teasing friend. Still, a feeling of pure contentment warmed her as she stared up at the high ceiling. Her lashes fluttered and another round of sleep seemed like a perfect idea.

Turning to her side, County snuggled deep into the crisp sheets and other soft coverings. She was about to close her eyes when they fixed on her phone book. Bolting up, she grabbed the book and the cordless phone from the brass nightstand.

"Stefan Lyons office, please," she requested when the switchboard operator inquired on how to direct her call.

"Stefan Lyons office, Sheila McPhereson speaking."

"Yes, this is Contessa Warren. I'd like to make an appointment to see Mr. Lyons."

"All right ma'am and may I ask what this is in reference to?"

County's smile was not humor induced. "This is in reference to his constant and aggravating offers to buy my publishing house."

"Please hold, Ms. Warren," Sheila asked after a few seconds of silence.

County propped her bed pillows behind her and hummed along to the O'Jays "I Love Music" for about forty seconds before Sheila returned.

"Will tomorrow at one be good for you, Ms. Warren?"

"That sounds perfect," County accepted.

"There will be lunch with Mr. Lyons in his office," Sheila explained.

County tossed her phone book back to the nightstand. "I look forward to it," she said and clicked off the phone.

Sheila wrote the date in Stef's appointment book and then looked up at the man himself who sat perched on the edge of her desk.

"That woman sounds like she don't play," Sheila noted, leaning back in her chair. "Are you sure about meeting with her? Especially since there won't be a sale resulting from it?"

Stef smiled and stroked his smooth jaw. "Only another man could understand the desire to meet with a woman who despises him so."

Sheila's brows rose. "Okay…" she sighed, reaching for her planning notebook. "So where would you like to have lunch ordered from?"

"You decide," Stef instructed, leaning forward to press his hand over hers, "before you do that though, call Fernando. This is one meeting he shouldn't miss."

"Please don't forget you share an office with your brother," Tykira gasped in her husband's ear.

"Who?" Quay asked, helping himself to the taste of his wife's ample breasts when they bounced before his face. His attentions to that and other areas of her anatomy had Ty crying out sharply as her fourth orgasm settled in.

Quay was relentless. He never ceased his thrusts

amidst her climax and loved the passionate picture she portrayed while straddling him on the chair behind his desk.

When they were both spent, Tykira cuddled close to Quay and her hair draped them in a lover's covering. "Are you gonna miss me when I'm gone?" she asked, kissing his temple.

"Don't ask dumb questions," he warned, absently trailing his fingers along the outside of her thigh. "I do have serious reservations about this trip of yours, though."

Tykira leaned back. "Why?"

"Because you won't let me come with you."

She nudged his nose with hers. "That's because you have your own business to handle. Besides, a break from all this steamy sex might do us some good."

"Mmm. Speak for yourself," Quay groaned, a contented look coming to his darkly gorgeous face as he leaned his head back on his chair.

Ty uttered a helpless sound, feeling him stiffen inside her again. She leaned forward in response to the powerful length beginning to fill her. "I meant, it'd make it even better when I get back from Denver."

"Damn Ty, could you just hush about Denver for a minute?" Quay asked, groaning as he held her bottom still for his thrusting.

Ty could barely get her words formed as she teased. "*Only* a minute?"

* * *

"Baby, do you want to meet at the restaurant for dinner?" Ty asked while fixing the belt at the waist of her coral wrap dress.

Quay sat watching her and cursing his arousal that was once again taking shape—literally. "We'll leave from home," he decided.

Tykira turned and fixed him with a knowing look. "Is that such a good idea?" she asked, sauntering closer to her husband.

Finally, Quay stood and put his own clothes in place. "What's wrong with that?"

"We may never leave the house," Ty predicted, laughing when he caught her wrist.

"I'm counting on it," he growled against her neck and began to kiss her jaw.

Another throaty kiss ensued, but Ty maintained a level head. She managed to wiggle out of her husband's embrace and blew him a kiss as she sprinted out of the door.

Quay watched her leave and then smiled. His eyes closed and he performed his daily ritual of thanking God for seeing fit to give him a life with Tykira Lowery.

"Yeah Jazz?" he greeted, when his phone buzzed some time later.

"Sorry Quay, but I've got a Lena Robinson on the line," Jasmine announced.

Mind alert, Quaysar thanked his assistant and

waited for her to patch the call through. "Hey Miss Lena," he greeted in the most humble manner.

"Quay, how are you?" In spite of her cordial response, it was clear that Lena Robinson wasn't eager to have the conversation.

"Miss Lena, thanks for returning my call and I won't keep you long," Quay promised, sensing the woman's reluctance. "I just wanted to know if you've seen or talked to Wake? I haven't spoken to him since late last year."

"Quay do you think I'm fool enough to give you people my son?"

"Miss Lena, I—"

"I gave Wake to you once before," Lena interrupted as sobs began to hinder her breathing, "I've regretted it ever since."

"Miss Lena? What—what do you mean?"

"Oh, Quay, I know you've always been a good friend to my baby."

"I still am, Miss Lena," Quay swore, his dark eyes narrowed with sincerity. "I'm not out to hurt him, Miss Lena. We all know who's really responsible for Sera Black, but we need Wake to corroborate certain things."

"Corroborate? Hmph. Wake has already put his life on the line too many times."

"With who? Marcus?"

Lena gasped. "How—?"

"When I talked to Wake, he reminded me about

how we met. When you came to interview with Uncle Marc… Anyway, *that* combined with the fact that Houston was responsible for Sera's death and Marc made it possible for certain pieces of evidence to remain hidden and Wake telling me he was a cleanup man and with your connection to Marc… Miss Lena, putting him and Wake together just seemed to fit." Quay silenced his lengthy explanation and prayed Lena would respond—confirm.

Shortly, the woman's light sobbing turned heavy. "That bastard Marc originally made me think Wake would just be running errands, things that could parlay into an internship or a good job with Ramsey afterward. The money was good. A little *too* good to just be doing errands. It wasn't until I saw him driving some woman around in one of Marc's cars that—" She stopped herself to take a deep breath. "It was one of your uncle's…women. Not his wife and that was just the tip of what I'd discovered. That's when I quit. But, I—I couldn't make Wake walk away. He'd never had money, but *all* his friends did and that's a tough thing for any child to grow up with or *without* so to speak," she cleared her throat and chuckled nervously. "When I finally realized what Marc was like, it was too late. Wake's hands were dirty—not as dirty as your uncle's but dirty enough to put my baby away and take his future."

"Miss Lena will you tell me about it?" Quay probed in his softest tone.

"I'm sorry Quay, but I won't," Lena's voice was firm. "My son has to live what little life he has and what I know...if Marc found out, he'd know it was me who told."

"Miss Lena, Marc's got way too much goin' on to think about that."

"Sweetie, are you talking about Houston?" Lena chuckled again. "Trust me, that devil has bigger horrors in his closet and you can best believe those horrors are still very much a part of his present. I won't do anything you hear me? *Anything* to bring more harm to my son."

"Miss Lena? Miss Lena?" Quay called, cursing softly when the dial tone sounded in his ear.

"Come in! Come in!" County called out when she woke hours later to heavy knocking on her bedroom door. "Oh, no," she groaned, dropping her face back into the pillow when Michaela's round face peeked inside past the door.

"Ooohwee," Mick noted with a playful glimmer in her amber eyes.

"Don't start," County ordered, her voice muffled.

Mick walked in. "Start what?" she asked, pressing the door shut and leaning back against it. "Start asking why you're all naked and tousled and *still* in bed at one p.m. or why I saw Fernando strollin' downstairs looking all smug and satisfied?"

County raised her head from the pillow. "If you weren't pregnant, I'd—"

"Please! County, this is great!" Mick laughed. "Fernando Ramsey is the last man I'd ever put you with, but now…"

"Go on," County urged, sitting up in bed and tucking the sheet around her.

"Honey look at you," Mick sighed, sitting next to her friend on the bed, "men fall to your feet like flies and it never causes you to bat a·lash. You walk into a room where Fernando is and you're like a flustered girl."

"Flustered girl," County repeated, her lips curving into a distasteful smile, "makes me sound weak and needy."

"Not weak and needy. Content and happy."

"Hmph," Contessa grimaced, fixing Mick with a sad look. "My nephew/niece is turning your brain to mush. You know, I read somewhere that women are prone to lose brain power the farther along they get in their pregnancy."

"Anyway," Mick retorted, rolling her eyes. "And what's with this nephew/niece thing? Don't you have a preference? Everyone else does."

"As long as it's healthy," County decided, spreading out the flared hem of Mick's burgundy tee where it lay on the bed. "And since my being the kid's auntie *and* godmother *still* doesn't merit me knowing its sex, nephew/niece is the best I can do."

Mick reached out to smooth a few tousled strands of County's hair. "Can't you be patient?"

County shrugged. "I just don't get all the secrecy."

Mick's easy expression grew somber. "I'm just hoping my girl will bring this family closer."

"Well she's gonna have to do a lot of work to—wait. What did you say? A girl? I'm gonna have a niece?"

Tears pooled Mick's eyes and she was only able to nod. She and Contessa laughed and cried while hugging tightly.

"I've been afraid of the sort of mother I'd make," Mick admitted, closing her eyes as she savored the hug. "I've been so scared that I'd make the same mistakes with her that my mother did with me."

County pulled back. "Not a chance." She swore.

Mick nodded. "I appreciate your certainty."

"Hell, yes, I'm certain. You're my best friend, aren't you?"

"What's that got to do with anything?"

County gave her a haughty look. "'Cause I don't make friends with idiots."

Again, laughter mixed with tears as another round of hugs began.

"You know I'm going to try talking you out of this more than once."

"And *you* know that I have to go," Fernando told Jeff Carnes that morning when they met in Jeff's office. "I have to see this for myself. It may be the only way to get my dad out of this family."

"What if you're recognized?"

Fernando clenched a massive fist. "I really don't think that'll happen."

"And if it does?"

"That's a chance I'll have to take."

Jeff regarded the powerful-looking young man seated before his desk. "I commend your bravery, son. I sincerely hope it won't get you killed. These are the sort of people we're dealing with," he said, seeing Fernando bristle. "They're evil, murderous sons of bitches and the fact that you're Marc's son will do little to protect you."

"Hmph, that's the one thing I *don't* need to be told," Fernando assured Jeff, grimacing at the sour taste that suddenly filled his mouth. "My dad put a crime ship in my name—his own son. Mr. J, I don't think there's much else that could surprise me."

Memphis, Tennessee

Wood Stanton smiled curiously as he leaned against the doorjamb and watched the cloud of fluffy black hair bobbing behind the desk.

"You okay?" he called out finally.

The jet-black cloud ceased its bobbing and rose as its owner peeked over the desk. Melina Dan's exotic black gaze narrowed even more when she produced a sheepish grin.

"Just a clumsy episode," she admitted.

"Need any help?" Wood offered, pushing himself

away from the door. Of course, Melina could've dropped a stick pin and had every man in the building ready to help her find it. Still, Wood wasn't surprised when she turned down his assistance.

"Thanks anyway," Melina called, her tone absent. Her fingers were poised over the spilled papers and the letter that had fallen from her desk drawer.

"Melina?" Wood called, noticing the look on her dark face.

"I'm okay, Wood," she said quickly, gathering the other papers and setting them atop her desk. "Seriously, I've got it covered," she assured, smiling when he nodded and left her office. Letting her easy look fade then, she stood behind the desk with the letter in hand. The French tips of her nails brushed across the envelope which bore only her first name scribbled across the front. She was seconds away from opening the envelope, knowing the contents by heart and knowing they would only torture her emotions for the millionth time. On cue, it seemed, her private line buzzed.

"Thank you," Melina whispered, setting the letter back to its resting place inside her top desk drawer. Clearing her throat, she pulled the phone from its cradle. "Hello?" she answered.

"Melina? This is Josephine."

"Sheila McPhereson."
County returned the smile to the woman who had

just introduced herself as Stefan Lyons's assistant. She'd just arrived for her appointment with Dark Squires and was more than ready for the meeting to commence.

"Right this way, Ms. Warren," Sheila said with a wave past her desk. "Mr. Lyons has been anticipating your meeting since you called."

"Well then, that's something we have in common," County said, smoothing both hands across the teal green asymmetrical skirt she wore with a white scooped neck tee. She hadn't bothered to dress in her most severe business attire for the meeting. Stefan Lyons was not someone she had any desire to impress. Besides, she wanted to be comfortable when she told the man to go to hell and take his bullying, scavenging piece of crap company with him.

The executive floor of Dark Squires vastly differed from its lower levels, which were accessible only by glass stairway to the fifth floor. A visitor had a breathtaking view of the starkly designed company offices and cubicles that housed the loud, fast-talking wheelers and dealers of all sizes and colors. Following Sheila McPhereson down the wing to Stefan Lyons's office, however, County could tell there would be none of that there. The soft hum of the cooling system could have been relaxing, except it wasn't. The luxurious carpet, thick and giving beneath the soles of her teal wedge-heeled sandals should have been inviting, but it only reminded her more of the calm before the storm.

Still, Contessa managed to maintain her smile regardless of how faint it was. Her eyes harbored unmasked suspicion and intensity as Sheila opened the doors leading to the office suite.

"Ms. Warren, it's a pleasure," Stefan greeted, already heading toward the door as though he'd seen her approach.

Probably has a camera in every corner of the place, County thought, barely raising her hand when Stefan moved in to shake it.

"That's all Sheila," he told his assistant without casting a look in her direction. "I hope you're hungry," he said to County, curving a hand beneath her elbow. "We have smoked salmon, wild rice, pumpernickel rolls, steamed asparagus and apple cake for dessert."

County nodded, her brown eyes focused as she let Stef lead her farther into the office. "It sounds wonderful, but you may want to hear me out before inviting me to break bread with you."

"Ms. Warren," Stef sighed, pressing a hand to the green and gold striped tie he wore with a dark forest green shirt, "can't we start fresh?" he proposed.

"Why? I still don't intend to sell," Contessa assured him, folding her arms across her chest. "And besides, your remarks to me on the phone practically begged for a more substantial response. I'm here to give you one."

Stef appeared as though he were trying to shield his humor by pressing his lips together as he cleared his throat. "Please do," he urged with a slight wave.

"You are an unprofessional jackass," she began without hesitation, leaning forward slightly to hold his eyes captive with her own. "You made your fortune off the backs of businesses already established and profitable. You're a parasite who gets even nastier when your *gracious* offers aren't welcomed with open arms. Yes, Mr. Lyons I've asked around about your company and I'm aware of your not so nice reputation."

"You don't get to be a success in this business by playing nice, Ms. Warren," Stef shared in a polite, albeit strained tone of voice.

County nodded as though she were agreeing. "Well, I suppose that would depend on a person's sense of ethics and *you* have the ethics of an alleycat scavenging anywhere he can find—whether it's already spoken for and off limits or not."

Stef's shoulders tensed beneath the worsted fabric of his suit. "In my defense of Dark Squires's interest in your House, it was my partner who was most determined in acquiring it."

"Mmm-hmm…"

"I swear to you, Ms. Warren," Stefan raised his hand, defensively, and then turned to head back toward the imposing desk at the rear of the office.

"However after I did my own…homework, I found that Contessa House was a very lucrative business. It would make a fine addition to this company."

"And where is this partner of yours?" County asked, while following Stefan deeper into the office. "Or is he too much of a coward to meet with me face-to-face?" she presumed.

The phone sounded then and Stefan raised his finger in silent request that County excuse him. He spoke only a few seconds with Sheila, before ending the call. "My assistant tells me my partner just entered the building and is on his way up now."

County only shrugged.

Stef clasped his hands and fixed her with a solemn smile. "I should apologize, Ms. Warren. I don't expect you to believe this, but speaking with you in person has certainly opened my eyes. I'm sorry that it hasn't done the same for my partner."

Blinking, County stepped closer to the desk. "Have I met with him before?" she asked.

Stefan put on his most convincing look of innocence. "According to the things he's said, I believe you might've," he shook his head. "It's like he was obsessed with taking your publishing house, but he knew it'd have to be done delicately because you were no fool. It'd take much wining, dining and other things he said he'd take great pleasure in, considering what a beauty you are. I'm sorry," he whispered when she blinked in obvious surprise, "it's just that my partner was very taken by you. He said that once he, um, *worked you,* was how he put it, you'd be willing to sign anything"

Contessa's lashes fluttered. "Bastards. The both of you," she spoke in a voice shuddering with contempt. "Just who is your partner to try and deceive me out of my business and God knows what else?"

A quick knock rapped on Stef's door before it opened.

"Ah, here he is now! Contessa Warren, this is my partner, Fernando Ramsey."

Chapter 13

Anyone who knew Contessa Warren well, knew nothing surprised her. Ever. If it did, she never showed it. Her heart didn't race, her eyes didn't widen and she was never afflicted by a sudden shortness of breath. It was the only reason her closest friends had never thrown her a surprise party.

In the time she'd known Fernando Ramsey, however, he'd managed to surprise her every time she was in his presence. She was almost beginning to think she'd know nothing but happy surprises where the man was concerned. *Told you Mick*, she mused silently.

"Well, I'm sure you two have much to discuss,"

Stef said, acting every bit the gracious host. "If you'll excuse me, I'll just—"

"Don't bother," County interjected, with a flip wave. "I'm leaving," she decided and braced herself as she headed towards the door and Fernando. Once there, she did her best not to touch any part of his massive, hard body.

Fernando's handsome caramel-toned face possessed the look of a lost little boy. He was helpless to think of anything to say. "County" was the most he could managed in a whisper. He reached for her arm, but she angled clear and left the office.

"Damn," Stef sighed, a satisfied smile on his face. "That's one fiery bitch."

Fernando's hands clenched into fists and he closed his eyes but a moment before turning to bound toward his partner. A second later, one of those massive fists smashed into Stef's face. The man yelped in pain, falling back against the corner of his desk.

"Dammit Fern!" he cried, through clenched teeth that were now crimson with blood. "You broke my damn jaw!"

Without a care for his partner's cries of pain, Fernando locked his hand around Stef's throat and squeezed. "Not yet, but don't worry, I'll be back to make it happen," he promised in the calmest of voices.

Fernando stormed out of the office, leaving Stef looking after him with a murderous stare.

* * *

"Dammit," County hissed, "come on," she urged, slamming her fist against the elevator buttons—praying one of the cars would arrive and save her from having to face Fernando again. No such luck, she realized, closing her eyes when she heard his deep voice rumble her name down the corridor. Giving up on the elevator, she headed for the stairwell. She was pressing down upon the door lever when he caught her.

"County stop," he urged, folding a hand over the lever and preventing the door from opening. "Let me explain," he pleaded when she snatched her hand from beneath his. His engrossing translucent brown eyes were filled with uncertainty and fear.

"There's no need to explain," County said when she turned to face him.

"You need to understand this," he said, taking hold of her upper arms as he leaned down to look directly into her deep brown eyes.

County blinked, sending a lone tear streaming down her cheek. "Why?" she asked, grimacing when she brushed away remnants of the tear. "Why now? Why now and why not before?"

"There was never a good time," he sighed in regret while his hands trembled slightly on her arms.

County rolled her eyes. "Not even when I told you what I knew about the ship?"

"County, it just wasn't—"

"The right time?" she challenged and nodded. "Let me go," she asked, eventually sounding defeated.

Fernando shook his head, his hold tightening. "Never," he swore.

"Fernando please, I—I need to get out—out of here. I can't hear you. I just can't hear you now."

"When?"

"I don't know."

"Can I call you later?"

County flashed him a despairing look. She had to get out of there—away from him and knew she wouldn't be in any more of a mood to talk to him later than she was at that very moment. Still, she nodded, hearing his sigh of relief. The second he released her, she dashed into an opening elevator car.

Quest smiled, sparking his deep left dimple. He inhaled the familiar honey-almond scent of his wife's glossy blue-black curls as his hands moved in slow, circular sweeps along her shoulder blades and spine.

Michaela snuggled her head deeper into the cushioning of the recliner they both shared.

"Hey, hey," Quest urged, patting his hand against her hip. "I don't know how long this chair can hold the both of us, so don't move around so much."

Mick shook her head. "The longer I'm pregnant, the worse your jokes get."

"I thought you liked my jokes?" Quest whined, pretending to be hurt.

Mick clenched her fist in triumph. "Yaay, I still have him fooled folks."

Quest pulled her back more tightly against him. "The minute the baby is born I'm carrying you off and giving you what you deserve," he warned.

Mick chuckled. "That'll be pretty tough, Pop, with a newborn screaming down the house."

"Ahh…my little girl will look out for me," he predicted.

"Is that right?" Mick sighed, contentment filling her voice and glowing on her dark face.

Quest nodded. "Mmm-hmm, I think she'll give me more than enough time to have my way with you."

Mick giggled and resituated herself to face her husband on the mammoth-sized black La-Z-Boy. "And what way is that, Mr. Ramsey," she taunted.

Quest simply cupped her cheek and held her still for his kiss. Simple pecks began to pepper Mick's lips, before his tongue outlined their fullness. She gasped, feeling his thumb rubbing her achy nipples beneath the soft cotton of her flaring lavender tee. The kiss deepened and was growing more heated when the front door slammed.

"County?" Mick called, seeing her friend hurry past the den door.

After a few moments, Contessa stuck her head inside the room. "Hey y'all," she greeted.

"Hey, you feel up to shopping and lunch?" Mick

asked, propping her chin on Quest's shoulder as she spoke.

County massaged her eyes. "Girl, I really just wanna stay in for the rest of the night."

Mick sat up a bit. "Are you okay?" she asked, finally tuning into the weariness surrounding her friend.

Suddenly, County broke into an uncharacteristic display of tears and waved her hand. "I'm sorry," she whispered, before racing upstairs.

"Hey, wait, wait a minute," Quest urged, when he saw that Mick was ready to go after her. "Give her a minute."

"Dammit Quest, didn't you see her crying?" Mick snapped, straining against his hold.

"I know, I know," he soothed, pressing a kiss to her cheek. "Just give her a minute to get herself together. Where's she going, but upstairs? Talk to her later, all right?"

Mick looked towards the den doorway, and then finally conceded with a quick nod. She resumed her place on the recliner and let her husband continue his massage.

After a long cry on the bed, Contessa washed her face and spent time overlooking the gorgeous backyard from her balcony. She called herself a fool at least fifty times. How in the world could she think Fernando Ramsey was the least bit interested or in love with her? How could he be, when she literally picked him up at a party, screwed his brains out and gave him an open invitation for more? No man in his right mind would turn down such an arrangement.

Now, she was angry because he'd lied to her? *Someone has to respect you before you can even expect truthfulness, County,* she told herself. Even then, it was still a hard thing to obtain. It was fun while it lasted and besides, she knew he'd been keeping something from her…so why did it still feel like her heart was shredding?

"Because you should be keeping your mind on business, idiot," she berated herself and grabbed her cell phone from the small round claw-foot table near the French doors. She smiled when the connection was made. Spivey's boisterous voice filtered through as he shouted orders to someone in the office before turning his attention to the phone.

"This is Spivey."

"Contessa here."

"Well hey!" Spivey called, chuckling at the sound of County's voice. "How's it goin' out there?"

"Fine, fine. Mick's good—big," County teased, joining in when Spivey laughed. "It sounds like you're busy?" she noted.

"Ah, a few slackers taking their time about shipping out some review copies. I had to crack down."

County shook her head over Spivey's playfully authoritative tone. "So what's new with our biggest upcoming release?"

"Well, I managed to wangle a few minutes to talk with the owner of the travel agency. The one responsible for getting the girls work on the ship," Spivey explained.

County nodded. "Can you get me on the ship?"

"I don't think that's such a good idea, County."

"Now Spivey—"

"Wait a minute," he urged softly, "just hear me out, all right? Now this slimy agency owner would only tell me that this ship is for men only. He made it clear that it was nothing a woman would want to be a part of."

"Unless you're working there, right?"

"It could be dangerous Contessa."

"Why don't you let me worry about that?"

"I don't like it."

"Spivey please. Look, whatever's going on out there, I need to see it for myself. So work on devising a ruse to get me out there—tell 'em I'm one of the new girls or something—"

"County—"

"Call me when I'm all set…Spive?"

"All right…all right, all right I'm on it," he promised.

Sighing once the connection broke, County tossed the phone aside and then resumed her gazing from the balcony. Her absent gaze softened when she heard the quick, insistent rapping on her bedroom door and the sound of Michaela's voice.

"County? Are you okay?" she whispered.

"Quest told me to leave you alone," Mick said when County opened the door. She glanced across her shoulder before easing into the room and shutting the door behind her. "I was worried, did something happen?"

"Not what you're thinking," County assured, pulling Mick into a hug. "I had a meeting at Dark Squires. They're the company trying to take the house."

"Dark Squires? Oh, no," Mick groaned and closed her eyes when she pulled out of the hug. "Fernando's company. And you didn't know?" she asked, watching County nod. "Oh, sweetie, I'm so sorry. I had no idea you didn't know that was his business."

"It's okay," County whispered and enveloped Mick into another hug. "I don't really want to talk about it, though. Is that okay?"

Mick looked into County's eyes and patted her cheek. "It's more than okay. You just take it easy, huh?"

"Mick?" County called, just as her friend prepared to step out of the room. "I don't want to talk to anyone."

Mick didn't need to be told who "anyone" was and nodded. "Get some rest," she ordered before leaving.

"To hell with it," Fernando muttered and continued on past the gates leading up to Quest and Mick's home. Contessa had told him she needed time, but he couldn't give her that. Besides, this was Seattle. She lived in Chicago. Hell, she already had distance—time was a luxury he couldn't afford.

He'd called himself a fool for not telling her about Dark Squires. After all their conversations, he couldn't find a way to ease in that choice bit of information. No wonder she thought he didn't respect her—had no use for her save the obvious.

Shaking the thought from his head, Fernando haphazardly parked his Ford F150 in the horseshoe drive, reached for his cellular and dialed the number.

"You good?" Quest asked, checking the temperature of the bubble bath he'd just run for his wife.

Michaela only smiled serenely as she eased down into the sunken gray marble tub. Her contentment was short-lived when the phone rang. Mick closed her hand over Quest's forearm when he rose to answer the call. "County doesn't want to talk to Fernando," she told him.

He only smiled, dropping a kiss to her forehead before he stood. "Relax and enjoy your bath," he ordered, deciding to take the phone in their bedroom.

"Hey man, I know she doesn't want to hear anything from me" were the first words Fernando spoke to his cousin.

"What the hell happened?" Quest asked, casting a quick look across his shoulder.

"Somehow, Stef arranged for her to have a meeting at Dark Squires. He made sure I was there."

Quest closed his eyes and grunted. "Hell, man, I always told you that fool was dangerous," he said, referring to Stefan.

"I wish I'd listened. Man, help me out here, all right?"

"Where are you?" Quest asked.

"Right outside your front door."

County had hoped a hot shower would soothe her nerves. It relaxed her body, but her mind was still a mess. She was finger-combing her short damp locks into place when a knock fell upon her door. Thinking it was Mick, she didn't hesitate to fling it open.

Fernando walked in before she could even think to close it.

"Does 'I need time' mean anything to you other than 'just come barging over when you feel like it'?"

"You knew I couldn't let it end that way," he said, his crystal clear brown gaze hard and probing.

County folded her arms across the bodice of the tie-dyed smock dress she wore.

Fernando took in her guarded stance. "I wouldn't be surprised to know you're thinking of hopping the first plane back to Chicago," he guessed.

County confirmed that he'd guessed correctly with a guilty look that was easy to spot. "Say what you came to say, and then let me be," she pleaded, turning her back toward him.

Bowing his head, Fernando slipped his hands inside the deep pockets of his light clay trousers. "You have to know I didn't do this to hurt you?"

"Do I?" County snapped, turning to face him then. "Do I Fernando? After all, it was me who practically said 'come home to bed with me.'"

"Dammit, can't you get over that?"

"I thought I could, until this."

"County—"

"What was it? Were you playing me or, as your partner said, *working* me, all along?" she asked, coming to stand right before him. "Did you want to see how much fun we could have before you tried again to persuade me to sell my business? Or maybe you thought after such good sex, I'd just give it to you? I'd sure as hell given you everything else."

"Dammit, Contessa, all right, I admit that when Stef approached me about the House, I was interested." He said, about to step even closer and then changing his mind. "I was also a little pissed that I hadn't thought of it myself. After all, acquiring Contessa House would be the perfect way to stifle Mick's book or *any* book on the family. Then, I met you and—"

"You just couldn't bear to take it and telling me the truth would've just hurt my little 'ol feelings?"

"No," he swore, this time taking the last step toward her, "No, after I met you, I wanted your

House even more," he confided, squeezing her upper arms and urging her to sit at the foot where he knelt before her.

"I wanted to bring it under Dark Squires wing, offer it more financial freedom."

"Financial freedom?" County spat haughtily. "My business is one of the top-grossing independent houses in the country."

"Bringing in what? Two, three million a year?"

"Yes, *and?*"

"And Dark Squires could help you gross five times that much."

"So then, all of a sudden you changed your mind?" County asked, refusing to be moved by his warm, enveloping voice and eyes.

Fernando's hands dropped from her arms to rest on either side of her on the bed. "I knew you better. We were…closer and I got scared that I'd lose you if you found out I was involved with the company. Besides, I knew you were happy with your business the way it was."

County straightened, her frown clearing somewhat. "Why would that matter to you?" she asked finally.

"Because taking a woman's dream isn't a good way to show you love her."

"Oh, why didn't you just tell me?" County sighed, remorse filling her voice. "Especially after I told you about the ship?"

"I had every intention of doing that very thing," he swore, "but then we found out about Houston and…everything just went off in another direction. But Contessa I meant everything I ever said to you. Everything. My feelings are real and I pray you can forgive me."

County stared helplessly at the ceiling. "I knew what we had was too wonderful. It takes time to craft something like that."

"Not always," he argued softly, his fingers brushing across her thighs bared by the hem of her dress.

Shaking her head, County reached out to toy with the gorgeous dark brown curls covering his head. "I constantly cursed myself for thinking there was something going on—something that would change things, but it was true. I don't blame you," she added, when he looked up. Her fingers fell to his jaw and she stroked his light shadow of his beard. "I enjoyed every bit of what happened between us, but all along I knew it would fizzle. I guess that's why I never let go of the mask," she said, flashing him a brief, sorrowful smile.

Fernando felt his jaw clench, knowing his temper was beginning its slow simmer. It was easy to read between the lines of her soft-spoken, sweetly painful words. They were telling him that she was about to end it and he couldn't listen to her say that.

Rising suddenly, he kissed her. County met the

force of the action with her own strength. Her hands cupped his face and she gasped, allowing him deeper into her mouth.

Their tongues battled passionately—furiously thrusting, encircling amidst an onset of desire, love and desperation.

Fernando ended the kiss, breathing harshly against her neck. "Don't leave without saying good-bye to me," he asked.

"I won't," she promised, squeezing her eyes shut against the tears filling them. "Besides, Mick'll kill me if I leave before the party," she said, attempting a lightness that wasn't forthcoming.

Fernando simply nodded, kissed her cheek and then he was gone. County watched the closed door for five seconds, before jumping up to beg him not to leave her.

Her cell phone chimed just as her fingers brushed the knob. Closing her eyes, she settled it within her mind that she and Fernando were too complicated, too driven by their desire for one another and all the forces that worked to make it impossible for that desire to flourish into more. Turning defeatedly, she answered the phone before it rang again.

"County?" Spivey called, at first not recognizing the lost sound in her voice.

She cleared her throat and forced the strength back into it. "What's up?"

"Your voyage on *The Wind Rage* is all set."

Chapter 14

Whatever tensions there may've been over the shower party, they fled with the arrival of the guests. Everyone seemed to be at ease and ready to enjoy the sunny afternoon weather. The party was an indoor/outdoor affair held at Quest and Michaela's home.

Classical jazz floated through the air as sweetly as the conversations that mingled throughout and focused mainly on the news that the couple would be delivering the first grandchild of the next generation—a granddaughter to the Ramsey clan. Food was plentiful and everyone was urged to feast until their hearts were content.

Surprisingly, Mick wasn't camped out by the buffet table. Instead, she stood looking over the gift table that teemed with brightly wrapped packages. She was about to give one a shake, when her hand was smacked. She gasped and looked up to see Quaysar's handsome face close to her own.

"Eek!" she squealed, hugging him tightly and then hugging Tykira. "Girl, thanks so much for getting him here."

"Hey," Quay complained, "it hurts me that you think I wouldn't come on my own."

Mick smacked his cheek. "Get over it. I should be mad anyway that you missed the announcement," she said, tugging on the sleeve of the white T-shirt he wore beneath a Supersonics jersey.

"Mick, I'm afraid that one's my fault," Ty admitted, squeezing her husband's hand.

"Oh, Lord," Mick drawled and waved her hand in the air. "I don't even wanna know."

"Well, we wanna know," Quay urged, patting his sister-in-law's growing tummy. "Spill it."

Mick cupped his face in her hands. "You and Ty can expect a little niece in the summer."

Quay closed his eyes and smiled before kissing Mick's palm. "A niece," he whispered, his dark eyes sparkling with warmth. "My very own little niece. I'm gonna have to teach her to be on the lookout for all the dogs out there." He looked as though he was making a to do list in his head.

"And I can't think of a better man to teach that subject," Mick laughed.

Quay and Ty joined in and soon the threesome was enveloped in a tight hug.

"Hey, hey, break it up!" Quest called upon his approach. "I wanna hug too."

The four were still hugging when Marcus and Josephine arrived. Conversation seemed to grow a smidge quieter throughout the crowded room. Quay's mood transformed as he left the hugging circle to stare down his uncle.

"Quay?" Ty called, taking her husband's hand and pressing it to the front of the deep turquoise halter blouse she wore. "Quay, please don't let this worry you. You knew we'd see him here, Quay," she called more forcefully when he didn't seem to tune in to her words. She made him face her.

Quay's ebony stare focused in on his wife's face and his anger seemed to melt. His hands spanned her waist and he pulled her into a throaty kiss.

Quest clapped his twin's shoulder. "Let's get somethin' to eat," he suggested and they headed for the buffet table with Mick and Ty close behind.

"What the hell are you doin' here?" Yohan demanded of Marcus.

"Han," Josephine whispered, rubbing her son's back to calm him.

Forgetting his father, Yohan turned and kissed his

mother's cheek. "You've made your appearance and set everyone on edge, rest assured," he said, keeping Josephine close to his side. "I'll make sure Ma gets home."

Marcus's eyes filled with momentary regret while watching his youngest child stroll off.

"Does it even bother you a little that all three of your sons hate you?"

Rolling his eyes at the sound of Damon's voice, Marcus turned. "Giving parenting advice now, Damon? I hope you haven't forgotten all the headaches those twins gave you?"

"They were children, what's your excuse?"

"Dammit, I'm not gonna stand here and let you preach to me from some soapbox!" he whispered viciously.

Damon only smirked. "It wouldn't do a damn bit of good anyway."

Marc stood clenching and unclenching his fists as his younger brother strolled away. Then he spotted Quest and Quay talking with Yohan across the room. His wicked juices rolled and coolly he strolled over to partake of the inviting buffet.

Mick found County alone on the patio enjoying the view. She rested her head against County's and dropped an arm across her shoulder. "Can I help?" she asked.

"No," County said and kissed Mick's temple. "I

just want to wallow in misery a little while longer and then I'll let it go."

"Mmm and how much of *it* are you talking about?"

"Mick, I don't know what's gonna happen between me and Fernando," County groaned, rubbing her arms through the sleeves of the coffee bean striped silk blouse she wore.

"Well, honey, is there any way you could forgive him and move past it?"

County laughed. "Mick I'm past it. It was business and I'm fine with letting go of that."

Mick slapped her hands to the sides of her bell-bottomed stretch jeans. "So what's the problem, then?"

"Mick, I don't—"

"Uh-uh, you've got to talk to me now."

Grimacing at being left with no choice, County pulled Mick aside. "Fernando has a strip club in Chicago—very posh, very affluent clientele. But several girls have been leaving the business. They've all gotten jobs on some cruise ship, for gentlemen only."

Mick shook her head. "Well that's not unusual."

"I have to know what's happening on that ship."

"Well damn girl, can't you figure that out on your own? Gambling, prostitution, drugs…on the open seas they wouldn't have to worry about much authority."

"Fernando says he didn't know," County whispered, massaging her eyes. "I want to believe him. I did believe him."

"But after Dark Squires you don't know?" Mick guessed.

County ran a hand through her hair and nodded. "I feel angry at myself for doubting him again, and I feel stupid because I'm letting my feelings blind me to what's right in front of my face. He told me his club was on the up and up, that as far as *he* knew, prostitution or anything illegal was nonexistent in his organization." She closed her eyes as though it were too much of a chore to keep them open. "If that's what's going on out there and he *is* involved, then there's truly no hope for us."

"Honey, you know Fernando, so you have to ask yourself if he could be involved in something like this."

"If I ask myself then the answer would be no and I'm afraid I don't much trust my judgment these days."

Suspicion filled Mick's amber eyes. "So how do you intend to find out? County, please tell me you're not going out to that ship?" she asked when County fixed her with a pointed look.

"Spivey was able to book me passage."

"Are you crazy?!" Mick raged, her eyes wide as small moons. "County that's dangerous, not to mention life threatening. Hell, that's only the sort of foolishness *I'd* pull."

"Well, since you're completely not in shape to

go—" County paused to pat Mick's tummy "—I have to. Besides, Mick, I have to know. I have to see for myself if there's anything *to* see."

"And if there's nothing to see?" Mick asked, her eyes narrowing. "Should I plan for another addition to the Ramsey family?"

"That's the one question I can't and *won't* answer," County decided, and then pulled Mick's hands into hers. "But I may have to leave the party early so please don't be upset if you happen to look up and find that I'm gone."

Michaela's gaze shifted momentarily before her arched brows rose a notch. "Leaving's going to be pretty tough since I'm sure Fernando will have his eyes on you the entire time."

County turned as Mick nodded. There stood Fernando several feet away talking with his cousins.

"Honey, just face him," Mick urged, with a calming smile. "Don't make any mad dashes. My secluded, romantic patio is your only escape anyway."

County opened her mouth to respond, when her eyes met with Fernando's. Of course, her first instinct was to retreat, but *of course* her feet wouldn't move. Mick simply patted her shoulder and left her standing there. Contessa swallowed, watching Fernando excuse himself from his cousins and head in her direction.

"I'm glad you didn't hop that plane without saying goodbye," he told her, once they shared the intimate patio.

County could barely make eye contact. His massive form completely blocked her view of anything going on inside the house. "I, um, was just telling Mick that I was going to have to say goodbye earlier than I expected."

Fernando made no comment. He simply watched her closely, his translucent browns seemed as though they were searing through the fabric of her shirt and caressing every curve beneath.

"I told her not to be surprised if she looked up and found me gone," she rambled on, focusing on the FUBU logo that was on his hunter green tee.

"Sounds important."

County nodded.

"Back in Chicago?" he called.

"No."

Fernando tensed, his body seeming to swell to twice its size. "Will you tell me where?"

"Fernando don't do this," she begged and shifted her weight from one foot to the other.

"So is it really business or are you just running from me?"

"It's not that," she said, surprised by the strength in her voice. "I have questions that need answers and to find them I have to take this trip."

Her words stoked curiosity within his striking eyes.

"Just don't ask me anymore questions," she begged, knowing he was about to do just that.

Fernando bowed his head, taking a few moments

to trail the back of his hand across his hair rough-ened jaw. "If I can't ask you questions then it's up to you to find a way to keep me quiet."

County rolled her eyes and fought the urge to smile. "How?" she asked.

"Dance with me."

A deep shiver raced through her. His simple request was about as innocent as a request to sit on his lap! Still, she nodded and accepted the hand he extended.

Lord, please don't let what I discover on that ship put an even deeper rift between us, County prayed, breathing deep as he stepped close. No man had ever affected her mind and body the way Fernando had. It would've been easy to resist his power over her body had her mind not been so intrigued by him as well.

They remained on the patio, alone and unnoticed amidst towering plants, vines and bushes. The music wafted in the air as though it were playing just for them. Fernando kept his intense gaze focused on Contessa's lovely honey-toned face. He judged her every reaction to his touch.

Every part of her body tingled. Especially that part of her that he'd taken such complete and unpar-alleled possession of. His steely arms wound tightly about her waist and sealed her against him.

Contessa scarcely wanted to rest her hands against his chest. The chiseled definition of his muscular torso produced a moan that ached to drift from her throat and mingle with the seductive music surrounding them. Weak, needy and not the least bit ashamed of it, she rested her forehead upon his chest.

Fernando lowered his hands from her back to envelope the full firmness of her bottom. There he squeezed, patted and caressed while nuzzling her neck and inhaling the airiness of her perfume.

County tugged her lip between her teeth, feeling the still subtle yet noticeable extent of his male length against her belly. She chanted a prayer that the song end soon, never realizing Fernando heard the barely audible pleas. County's moan left her throat when his lips and tongue nibbled the flesh at her neck.

"Stop," she asked, her breasts heaving fiercely against him as his fingers massaged beneath her shirt at the small of her back.

"May I ask my question?"

"No," she refused, feeling his tongue invade her mouth a half second later. Her hands curved into fists that pounded his chest in a futile and purely phony show of resistance.

They lost themselves in the seclusion of the patio. Fernando allowed his hands and mouth free rein across her body. County arched her breasts into his palms and thrust her tongue desperately against his when his thumbs barely brushed the nipples rigid and begging for more attention.

"Mmm," she moaned helplessly. Any thoughts of

resisting were distant memories and a surge of power rushed her when she heard him utter a similarly helpless moan.

Fernando effortlessly carried her to an even more private area of the patio. Keeping her trapped against the brick wall, his big hands splayed across her thighs in a possessive fashion. Torturing her without mercy, his fingers rubbed her femininity through the crotch of her jeans. County broke the kiss to rain tiny wet pecks along his whiskered jaw and neck. Her blatant desire aroused him so, that the need to take her then and there overruled any other coherent thought.

The charged moment, however, thundered to a halt at the sound that caught their ears and widened their eyes.

"What was that?" they asked in unison.

"Quay please don't do this," Ty whispered, frantic as she grasped her husband's arm. "Sweetie, not here," she urged, gripping the collar of his jersey which threatened to tear under the pressure of his resistance.

"Let me go, Tyke," Quay ordered, his black gaze fixed on Marcus Ramsey.

"Honey, please—"

"Ty!"

Tykira released her hold on his shirt and looked around for a sign that anyone heard the commotion and was coming to Marcus's rescue. Miraculously, no one seemed to have paid attention to the crash of the small table that carried the large cut glass punchbowl or matching glasses. Ty spotted Fernando and Contessa coming in from the patio and hurried over to them.

"What happened?" County asked.

"Marc said something to Quay and he went crazy," Ty explained, clasping both hands to the front of her turquoise halter. "Fernando, please stop this," she cried.

"Shh," he soothed, taking her hands and giving them a gentle squeeze, "it's all right. Besides, don't you think Quay's entitled?"

Twin expressions of disbelief emerged on Contessa's and Tykira's faces.

"Fernando!" they cried simultaneously.

Ty moved on, desperate to find someone to stop Quay who, by now, was muttering something to Marc that was no doubt life threatening. Meanwhile, County continued to study Fernando.

"He's your father," she reminded him gently.

"And he deserves whatever he's got coming from Quay."

"How can you say that? You act like it was Marc who killed Sera."

Fernando stood with one arm folded across his chest, one hand cupped beneath his arm while the other stroked his beard. "He's done enough to my brothers, my mother, me…"

"Will you tell me?" she asked, curving her hand over his forearm as she witnessed the glimpse of uncertainty in his gaze. "You think I'd use it against you?" she guessed.

Fernando turned the tables and clutched Contessa's upper arms in his massive grasp. "I'm about this close—" he tugged her forward "—to losing you and if you think I'm gonna tell you anything—" he stopped when she blinked in surprise.

"There's more isn't there? More secrets?"

"A man like me has plenty of secrets. Many that are better just left buried."

"And this is why we're at a standstill, don't you see?"

"And there are some things I never want you to have to deal with. Now if you can't accept that, County…"

County's lips parted and she stepped away from Fernando. She watched him as though he were a stranger. Suddenly, the sound of more heated voices overshadowed all other conversations in the room.

"You and your brother never could control your tempers!" Marc raged, straightening his tie while eyeing the twins with unmasked disgust. "Especially you, Quay!" he accused and pointed a finger at his younger nephew. "You don't waste a minute to show your ass the first chance you get!"

"And you believe I care what you think of me?" Quay bellowed, his hands spread as he shrugged. "Hell, you harbored a murderer and have somehow managed to weasel out of payin' for it! But I guess that's small potatoes to you, huh? I guess you just add that to all the other crap you've pulled over the years. I bet Aunt Josie could probably give us an earful on what a sorry bastard of a husband you are!"

"Quest, please stop this before it goes too far," Ty begged, clutching the front of the deep purple T-shirt emblazoned with the Greek letters of his fraternity.

Glancing at his watch, Quest shrugged. "Well, I promised him at least fifteen minutes to go at Marc before I stepped in."

"Quest!" Tykira and Mick cried in unison.

"A sorry husband?" Marc threw back at Quay, pure wickedness fueling the smile on his face. "Hell son, your only experience with women is seeing how many you can screw and dump in a week," he noted and cast a leering look toward Tykira. "She's quite a piece of eye candy but once you've had your fill, you'll dump her, too—wife or not."

"Son of a bitch!" Quay hissed, blind rage blocking any sense of restraint he might've had. "Because of you," he breathed, gripping Marc's jacket lapels so tightly they ripped, "you and your jackass brother, we went through hell."

Marc simply rose a brow. "I see and is that how you justify treating that beautiful girl like a slut you banged and threw away?"

Quay roared something vicious and indecipherable as he lit into Marc. His fist crashed squarely into his uncle's cheek and repeated nonstop. Contessa begged Fernando to step in, while Mick and Ty pleaded with Quest. Josephine tried to push Yohan to do something. Even Damon and Westin were reluctant to intervene on their brother's behalf. Quay followed Marc to the floor and continued to pound away at his face.

Quest finally decided to get involved. Unfortunately, he found it almost impossible to pull his twin off their uncle. Luckily for Marcus, his eldest son was just arriving for the party. Moses hesitated but a moment when he witnessed the scene, before going to assist Quest. Together, they managed to pull an infuriated Quay off Marc. Quay roared obscenities as his brother and cousin dragged him down one of the corridors leading from the sunroom where the guests had gathered.

"Get the hell off me! Dammit…I'm not done!" Quay raged, punching at Moses's forearm where it lodged beneath his neck.

Quest nodded for his cousin to let go once they were safely tucked away in his study. Quay made a dash for the door, but his brother held him fast.

"Let it go, let it go," Quest whispered, his arms locked around Quay's torso as he spoke the words against his ear. "Come on, that's it…" he soothed, feeling his twin's breathing slow. When a few moments passed, Quest released his hold and caught his own breath. "Thanks man," he said to Moses.

A playfully uncertain grin crossed Moses handsome blackberry face. "And here I was feeling bad about coming to tell you what I knew—thought I'd be putting a damper on a sweet family gathering," he added in a sarcastic manner.

"What are you talkin' about?" Quay asked, as he sat massaging his hands. "What do you know?"

Moses's playfulness vanished as he fixed his cousins with solemn looks. "Wake Robinson is dead."

Chapter 15

"Are you sure?"

"How?"

"When?"

Such were the questions thrown at Moses when he announced Wake's death. By that time, Quest's study was filled by Mick, Ty, Yohan, Fernando and Contessa.

"I'm positive," Moses answered Mick, dropping an arm across her shoulders and pressing a kiss to the top of her head. "After the incident on the train, my team kept an eye out hoping Wake would surface. One of my guys caught up to him just as the accident happened."

"Accident?" Mick queried.

"Some kind of freak explosion," Moses explained,

taking a seat next to Quay on the sofa. "Wake had the cops on his ass."

Again, stunned silence filled the room.

"Cops?"

Moses leaned forward, bracing his elbows to his knees while massaging his bald head. "There was a chase that ended at some warehouse when he rammed into it with his truck." Moses leaned back on the sofa. "Next thing the cops knew, the truck had gone up in flames. It destroyed the building, the truck...Wake."

"Are they sure it was him?" Ty asked.

Moses nodded. "My guy out there made visual contact just before the chase headed out to the freeway. As far as I know, the authorities haven't uncovered anything more binding—no dentals, no nothing."

"Why were the cops chasing him?" County asked.

"That's the crazy part of it," Moses assured with a grimace. "It was some stupid traffic violation—he ran a red light or something."

"That *is* crazy," Quest said from the spot he occupied behind his desk, "why would he do something to bring attention to himself like that?"

"Are they sure it was an accident?"

Silence filled the room as everyone turned to Fernando who had voiced the question. Then, at once, they all looked to Moses for answers.

"They honestly don't know, man," Moses told his brother and stood. "But my guess is that it was anything but an accident."

* * *

Michaela had intended for her shower party to be a weekend affair with everyone staying over and making it a two day event. Circumstances made that impossible. Marc left the party without Josephine. In spite of his injuries, no one knew or cared where he'd gone. Damon and Catrina took Josephine home with them for a change of scenery and to give her a breather from her husband. The group was reeling from the news of Wake's death. Now, they had a new mystery on their hands: had Wake been murdered? If so, by whom, why and why now?

Fernando left with his brothers that night and Contessa was glad. She needed to be focused on the situation at hand. She couldn't afford to let her emotions be swayed anymore by her feelings.

"Would you please cheer up? I'll be fine." County tried to assure Mick who'd been grilling her about taking the trip, for the better part of the morning.

"I just don't like this," Mick said skeptically, eyeing the cab that waited for County. "There has to be another way."

County took Mick by the shoulders. "Listen to me. This is information that I don't want second-hand. I have to see it for myself."

"What you'll see is what I'm afraid of," Mick grumbled as they hugged. "Are you sure about this plan of attack you and Spivey concocted?"

"Well, I better be, because we don't have time to change it," Contessa sighed, taking her overnight case as she and Mick descended the wide front porch steps.

Mick pushed her hands into the side pockets of her tangerine and white sundress. "Are you sure they'll let you on the boat—it being a gentleman's ship and all?"

"Spivey and I are a powerful couple with lots of money to spend," County reminded Mick, speaking of the ruse they'd devised for their cover, "woman or not, those folks ain't about to turn down those sorts of high rollers," she said, smiling as the cab driver went to place her bags in the trunk.

"Just keep Spivey in your sights at all times," Mick cautioned, blinking tears from her eyes when she and County hugged again.

County promised to do so and then pressed a kiss to Mick's cheek. Soon, the cab was rolling down the brick drive on its way to the airport.

Meanwhile, Fernando was having the same *think twice before you do this,* speech with his brothers. Moses, who seemed to fear nothing, thought it was a good idea for his brother to go and only wished he could tag along. Yohan was just as fearless, but took note of their father's evil tendencies. Clearly, Yohan preferred his brother staying alive to having him out gathering evidence against their father.

* * *

"My mind's made up," Fernando said as he snapped the last two locks on his suitcase. "I gotta do this Yo," he told his younger brother, clapping one hand to his shoulder. "That ship is partly in my name which means whatever's going on out there is my responsibility. Hell, I thought I was done lying to Contessa," he grimaced, stroking his beard out of frustration. "But this, I don't know if I could tell her about this."

Yohan smiled knowingly. "You love her."

Fernando's grin crinkled his eyes at the corners. "Heaven help me I do. In only a few months time I've gone and fallen in love with a woman who's completely unlike any woman I've ever met and I'll do anything to keep her."

"You know if her House is working on this book, there's a good chance this'll come out." Yohan cautioned, folding heavily muscled arms across the front of the brick short-sleeved Karl Kani T-shirt he wore. "Then, you'll have to explain why you kept another secret."

"Hell, Yo, how am I supposed to tell her something like this? Especially when she already thinks this family's scum?" Fernando questioned, searching his brother's face for answers he desperately wanted to hear.

"This is Pop's dirt, not ours," Yohan corrected. "If you try to hide this and it comes out, even *that* won't matter."

Fernando's light gaze hardened. "I don't want to talk about this, Yo."

Yohan nodded, decided to let the matter rest. "As long as you understand that Contessa Warren isn't a woman you can just pat on the bottom, give a diamond bracelet to and then send her on her way when she starts asking too many questions."

Fernando stroked the crisp whiskers shadowing the lower half of his face. "I know," he admitted, closing his eyes. "I think that's why I want her so damn bad."

Kauai, Hawaii

Cufi Muhammad was a picture of proud success. He'd made a living out of what many would have deemed a scandalous profession, but the arrogant South African decided he was providing a service— a service he was well paid and well envied for.

He nodded toward the arriving passengers, hands in the pockets of the elegant white quarter-length suit coat he wore with matching trousers. Cufi strolled the deck of *The Wind Rage* as though he were the king of a country.

Several faces he recognized—a few were new referrals from one or more of his many European and Asian contacts. However, it was the Americans whom Cufi was most anxious to meet. Aside from his partner Marcus Ramsey and his contributions to the business, Cufi had required little American par-

ticipation in the other aspects of his organization.
He'd never had an American client and had steered
clear for fear that it could lead to disastrous results.

Of course he'd had Warren Frinks and Joseph
Simon thoroughly checked out. Frinks and Simon
held connections that might increase his business ten-
fold.

Cufi's small, close-set eyes narrowed. He'd
spotted the big man who towered over almost
everyone he passed. He was younger than expected,
Cufi noted. Still, that could definitely be to his advantage. Engaging an older man in such a venture
could be quite difficult as experience had taught
him.

"Mr. Simon?" Cufi called, smiling more broadly
when the young man nodded and headed toward
him.

"Cufi Muhammad," he announced once they were
shaking hands. Fernando, who decided to use his
mother's maiden name and the male version of her
first name, cast an approving glace at his surroundings.

"Quite a vessel. Must be a challenge running it,"
he predicted.

"You have no idea, son," Cufi agreed, his round
dark face beaming with pride. "I wouldn't trade that
challenge for anything. My silent partners allow me
to staff *The Wind Rage* with the best people, thus
making my job much easier. I have every luxury at

my fingertips," He paused, to gesture around the main deck complete with glistening cherrywood floors and lounge chairs that were lined with silken cushions.

"And may I assume that the gambling aspects are just as luxurious?" Fernando inquired, casually easing one hand into the pocket of his cocoa trousers.

Cufi chuckled. "Luxurious doesn't begin to describe it, son. You'll have an endless selection of games at your disposal." He said, drawing Fernando closer. "The same is true for the women. My people *did* inform you about the women?"

Fernando bowed his head, stroking his beard in an effort to hide the distasteful grin on his lips. "I know about the women," he confirmed, raising his striking gaze to Cufi's face. "I hope that selection will be just as impressive?"

Cufi rubbed his hands together. "A breathtaking selection. I can assure you of that—all shapes, all sizes…all ages."

Fernando's chin rose. "Ages?" he prompted.

"As firm and as young as sixteen," Cufi taunted, complete delight in his voice, "of course, if you require younger treasures that will cost you and, of course, I don't travel with them."

"Of course," Fernando replied, swallowing the bile flavoring his throat. "But that won't be necessary. I prefer my women more experienced."

Cufi nodded and clapped Fernando's back.

"Then, I'm certain you'll find just what you're looking for."

The sound of Cufi's voice, his grinning face and friendly pats to his back, were slowly fueling Fernando's anger. He could feel the low rumble in his chest as his fists clenched—telltale signals that he was seconds away from losing his temper. Cufi had turned to speak with one of the pursers and Fernando used the opportunity to take deep, refreshing breaths. He ran a hand across his face and looked up to see something that set his temper back to simmer.

"Jesus," he hissed, then remembered Cufi and turned to see that he was still involved with the purser. Satisfied that the man would be thoroughly occupied for a while, Fernando left his side.

"Dammit," Contessa hissed, when the ringing cell phone interrupted her search for Spivey across the crowded deck. "Yes?!" she snapped into the receiver.

"Contessa!"

"Spivey? Dammit where are you? I'm looking all over this place and I can't—"

"Chicago!"

County felt her heart sink. "What the hell? What are you still doing back there?"

"What happened to us leaving from Chicago and arriving in Hawaii together?" Spivey wanted to know.

"It made more sense to just go on and leave from

Seattle," County sighed, the gorgeous view of turquoise skies forcing no improvement on her mood. "I know the ship doesn't sail 'til in the morning, but this would give us more time to investigate."

"You could've told me about this little change in plans, County."

"Spivey really. What difference does it make now? What I want to know is why you're still in Chicago and not flying through the air on your way to Hawaii?"

Spivey hesitated. "I found out more information on the ship."

"So? Tell it to me when you get here. I'll keep up the cover and head on to the cabin."

"The cabin? County where are you?"

"I'm at the ship. I'm standing on the main deck talking to you right now."

"Jesus…"

"Spivey what's wrong with you?!"

"I want you to turn around and walk off that boat right now!"

"After all the scheming we did to get on this son of a bitch? Hell, no!"

"County—"

"Listen Spivey, I don't know what's going on, but there's no way I'm gonna turn and leave just because—"

"Dammit Contessa!"

Blinking slowly, County gripped her phone a bit

more tightly. "Spivey? Spivey what's going on? What's wrong?"

"They're slavers, County," Spivey said after taking several deep, calming breaths. "They drug and abduct women, get them on that ship and then it's off to parts unknown."

County pressed her lips together to stop their sudden trembling.

"Somehow they lure 'em in with the promise of a great lifestyle, travel, financial freedom…that probably explains how your boy's strippers got there. Once they realize what's going on, it's too late. There's no way out."

County was cold all over and stood there wishing she'd listened to Mick. *Keep it together Count*, she ordered herself. "How did Marc Ramsey keep this hidden?" she asked.

"He's a partner," Spivey explained. "Only one top dog is actually hands-on. He works directly from the ship."

"I assume he'll be my host for the trip."

"No. No County he won't because you're bringing your ass back to Chicago. Now!"

"Spivey please listen to me. There's no way I can leave undetected now," she said, taking note of the fact that the deck teemed with men—something that, under different circumstances, would have delighted her.

"Damn, damn," Spivey moaned, "if only I'd gotten my hands on this information sooner. Listen,

I'm gonna have that boat tracked down and get you out of there one way or another."

"Spivey wait! Just wait a minute. Give me some time to think, all right?"

"Hell, no! Hell, no, County! Dammit it was risky enough you being there with me. Without me there, uh-uh. Look just drop everything and run like hell."

Surprised by her calm, County stood there trying to ease Spivey's worries when she felt her arm taken in a steel grip. She gasped sharply and turned to look right up at Fernando. Her heart dropped to her toes and she could barely hear Spivey calling out to her.

"Hello?" Fernando spoke into the phone after taking it from County's weak hand. "This is Fernando Ramsey…hey Spivey. Yeah…yeah. Listen she's fine…long story…yeah. She'll be with me and I'll make sure she gets off the boat and back home. You've got my word," he said, and then recited his cell number to Spivey and ended the call.

County propped one hand to her hip. "Your word? Ha!"

"Shut up," he muttered, his light eyes now darkened with fury. "What the hell are you doing here?" His deep voice rumbled.

County wasn't intimidated when he blocked her view with his massive frame. "You jackass. I could ask you the same thing. Just checking out the business, right?" She sneered, raising her hand when he opened his mouth. "Save it. Don't bother telling me you had no idea this was going on. I believed that lie once—never again," she said, shaking her head slowly.

Fernando rolled his eyes and then turned to snatch Contessa's garment bag from the porter who approached. "Come with me," he growled to County before hissing a sharp curse as Cufi Muhammad arrived at their side.

"Mr. Simons and a very lovely friend," Cufi noted, clapping Fernando's arm while he looked on in interest. "Surely as experienced as she is candy to the eyes," he drawled.

Fernando bowed his head to hide the dancing muscle when he clenched his jaw. He had to shove his fist deep within a trouser pocket, lest it smash the man's gut.

County took an instant dislike to the man's small, leering gaze especially when he spoke the words "very lovely" again and reached out to trail his index finger across her cleavage outlined so prominently at the halter bodice of the curve-hugging tangerine frock she wore. She stepped to make an angry lunge for the fiftysomething man and was immediately restrained by Fernando's iron grip.

Cufi chuckled heartily—yet the sound was more unsettling than it was humorous. "Feisty," he noted, his eyes appraising her face and heaving bosom. "Must be one of Marc's last-minute additions. He always provides me with my fiery Americans," he saw fit to explain to Fernando. "Still," he added, curving his right hand around County's jaw, "I'm surprised he sent her here unsupervised," he mentioned, and then patted her waist and sought to bring her close. "Give me a moment to get her calm," he decided.

Fernando held County fast. "What time is dinner?" he asked.

Cufi's hand fell away from County. "Five hours. Why do you ask?"

Smirking wickedly, Fernando fixed Contessa with a leer of his own. "I'll take this one as is. Breaking her in will work up my appetite."

County felt her legs turn to rubber, but still cringed and fought against Fernando as he pulled her away with him. Cufi's laughter roared in the air.

Contessa spoke barely a word as they headed to Fernando's cabin. Of course, much of her silence had to do with shock. Everywhere there was a scantily clad woman with a blank look in her eyes and a half smile on her lips. Everywhere there was a man with his hands or mouth somewhere on a woman's body. The blatant sexual displays shocked even her.

Fernando halted his steps behind the porter who escorted them. His grip tightened over the gold bracelet that hugged County's upper arm. It was a warning squeeze and County swallowed—not knowing if she would've been safer out on the main deck or inside his room. The porter opened the door and Fernando, giving her a slight nudge, forced her inside the spacious, impressively designed cabin suite.

County took in the luxury of the cabin while Fernando tipped the porter. Her brown gaze was absent and not the least bit moved by her surroundings. She was massaging her arm where Fernando had held her, when she heard a loud rumble and saw that her small case had been slammed against the wall. Whirling around, she blinked at the angry glint filtering his translucent stare.

"What the hell are you doing here?" His voice grated as he stalked her.

"Don't bother telling me this isn't what I think it is," County sneered, stumbling over the high wedge heels of her strappy gold sandals as she backed away from him. Her heart sank down to her stomach when she witnessed his expression grow more menacing. Soon, she'd run out of room to retreat. "No rebuttal, Ramsey? Or are you too busy thinking up a lie, you son of a bitch?!" she hissed, using her words as weapons.

At last, Fernando had completely blocked her in the far corner of the living area. "This is *exactly* what you think it is," he whispered.

County swallowed. "A slave ship."

"Tsk, tsk, tsk," Fernando gestured with a lazy

shake of his head. "Those words have such ugly connotations, Contessa. I prefer Ship of Delights."

County took in the breadth of his massive chest beneath the black silk shirt he wore. She focused on the chords of his neck visible as the collar of his shirt was left undone to reveal the gold herringbone chain he wore. Overwhelmed by the size and strength of him, she silently commanded herself not to faint.

"You make me sick," she breathed.

"Hmph," he remarked, setting his hand lightly upon her hip. "I promise you'll change your tune."

"I prayed that I would be wrong about you, but I guess I wasn't," she said to herself.

Fernando allowed his regret to show when she bowed her head in defeat. He cursed the fact that she followed her clues and had been led there. He knew that behind her still fierce demeanor that she was most definitely afraid. Unfortunately, it was too late to ease her fears now. He decided he would have a better chance of controlling her and protecting his cover if she were afraid. It would be the best way to keep her alive.

"Dammit, stop crowding me!" she snapped suddenly, and eased away through an open sliver of space.

Fernando caught her wrist and set her to the bed. "What'd you expect to find here?" he roared.

County curved her nails into the black velvet comforter. "Not this," she admitted.

Fernando clenched a fist. "Fool. Do you know what kind of people you're dealing with?"

"I thought I did."

Fernando braced his huge fists on either side of County on the bed. "I'm still the man you've been sleeping with for the last three months."

"I'm about to vomit."

"Really?" he whispered. His deep voice was soft and lightly playful. His nose trailed her temple, down the slope of her nose and then the curve of her cheek.

County closed her eyes and begged herself for the ability to remain unresponsive. She blinked and focused on the ceiling when one of his hands cupped her breast and his thumb assaulted the nipple with airy circles around the firm tip. She swallowed a moan when the walls of her sex contracted in response to the sweet sensations his touch invoked.

Fernando was just as affected and driven by the need to touch her. However, he knew he couldn't allow those needs to cloud what had to be done.

"Do you have any clothes for dinner?" he asked, reluctantly moving his hand from her body.

"I packed light," she answered softly. "Conservative," she saw fit to add.

Fernando grimaced. "That won't do. How the hell did you even get on a ship for men only?"

Some of County's fear dissipated. "Come on, Ramsey," she sighed. "Clearly that's not true. Spivey—using the name Warren Frinks—was to travel on board as a high stakes gambler. I was going as his companion," she explained.

"Stupid," Fernando muttered, rising to his full height while rubbing a hand through his dark brown curls. "Well, you can't go to your cabin because Muhammad wants to meet his other American client."

"Sick. All of you," County sneered.

Fernando felt on the verge of vomiting himself, but knew he had a better chance of Contessa keeping her mouth shut if she was suspicious of him. Ironic, he thought, he'd wanted her to trust that he was being real with her and now he wanted her to believe just the opposite.

"We should get you some extra clothes," he suggested, checking inside his jacket pocket for his wallet. "Come," he said, curling a hand around her arm once more.

County tried to wrench herself free. "I'm staying here," she snapped.

"I'm sure your plan wasn't to stay in the cabin the entire time," he challenged and jerked her close. County kept her balance by resting her hand against his chest and he smiled. "Unless, you were planning to sneak around undetected by disguising yourself as a man? Which, by the way, is something you couldn't do no matter how hard you tried."

Again, County tried to wrench free of his hold.

Again, he jerked her close. "If you plan to leave

this boat with your life and health intact, you'll do exactly what I tell you. No arguments." He brought his face close to hers then. "Disobey me, County, and you'll be very sorry."

County searched his striking gaze. In her heart, she knew he'd never hurt her—not physically anyway. There was more to this. A part of her knew she had to stay—had to get as much information as possible. She had to talk with some of the women. Most importantly, she had to find a way to put an end to this ship of horrors which, she regretfully acknowledged, would quite possible destroy the man she loved.

Chapter 16

Contessa appeared as though she were a child viewing some great wonder while she was being escorted along the corridors and decks of *The Wind Rage*. Exotic music—erotically mesmerizing—seasoned the air. Couples lay sprawled in lounges, along the pool—anywhere there may've been an empty space.

How could this exist? She asked herself. Numerous times she wondered how the authorities hadn't discovered such a thing. Sadly, she admitted *such a thing* may be more common than she realized. She shivered at the possibility.

Fernando felt her shudder and rubbed his hand along her bare arm. "Cold?" he asked.

"Go to hell," was the prompt reply.

Her reaction was due simply to all she'd discovered, Fernando told himself. Still, it stung. Setting his jaw in a hard line, he prayed for the strength not to break down and confess everything to her then and there and delight himself in seeing the love in her eyes again. Long lashes closed over his deep-set gaze and he told himself to let go of such a boyish fantasy. This was all too real and it could become all too deadly with just one misspoken word.

They stepped into a posh-looking boutique at the end of an upper level along the grand lobby of the ship. One of the male associates spotted them instantly and headed over.

Fernando turned to County, curving one massive hand around her throat, forcing her to look up at him. "Rule number one *and only*—don't call me by name," he said.

A hateful smirk curved her full lips. "That should be easy since all I want to call you is son of a bitch, jackass and bastard."

Unconsciously, Fernando tightened his hold around her neck.

"Ramsey," she gasped.

The hold loosened, but Fernando's expression had grown even more fierce. Clearly, he awaited a suitable reply to his instructions.

County rolled her eyes. "I'll remember," she whispered.

"Good," he said, tightening his hold about her throat once more and pulling her into a lazy, deep kiss.

Totally unprepared, she moaned and instinctively arched into his chiseled frame. She'd barely begun to thrust her tongue against his, when he broke the kiss.

"What a couple!" the sales associate commended, folding his arms over the fitted crew shirt that was supposed to add definition to his bony torso. "We rarely see such a match," he added.

Fernando barely nodded, before motioning toward Contessa. "Do you have anything gorgeous enough for a body like this?" he asked.

The associate's eyes lingered on County's face and apparently he adored what he saw. Then, he looked down and seemed even more enthralled by the body that went along. "Damn, baby, are these real?" he inquired, making a move to grope her bosom.

Fernando held County back and caught the associate's hand in an awkward grip that sent the man shrieking in pain.

"Why don't we start with the evening dresses," he suggested, intermittently clearing his throat and massaging the ache from his wrist. "What sort of event are we preparing for?"

County cringed, listening to the men speak about her as though she had no mind or mouth to speak for herself. Fernando knew her size and the color she favored. The fact shocked her, but she refused to let it go to her head. What she needed to know was why he didn't want her to speak his name.

The associate walked away to make a few selections and Fernando turned to wave toward the array of dresses.

"See anything you like?" he asked.

County regarded him with a scathing look. "No. You haven't dropped dead yet."

Fernando muttered a curse. "You know this would be a lot easier if you'd just cooperate with me."

"Kiss my—"

"Ahhh!" The sales associate raved upon his return. "I've taken the liberty of making a few choices. I think any of these would purely adore such a sensuous frame."

The associate led them to the dressing rooms. He offered to assist Contessa, but reconsidered when Fernando fixed him with a murderous glare. "Well, the rooms are spacious enough for two," he implied while unlocking the door.

Fernando was already leading her toward the rooms, but County moved before him and pressed her hands to his chest.

"Haven't you humiliated me enough? I'll try on

the clothes and come out here for you to see. I'll wear whatever you like best," she said.

"Hmmm…cooperative in bed and out," the associate noted, making himself scarce when the couple stared him down.

"Please Ramsey," she whispered when they were alone.

Fernando couldn't refuse her. His gaze softened and he brushed his thumb along her cheek, and then favored her bottom lip with a few teasing brushes. He nodded, uttering a curse when she was gone.

It didn't take long for County to change in and out of the outfits. Fernando could've cared less about what was chosen—they were all stunning on her. He experienced joy and torture watching her twirl around for him in one sexy creation after another. Finally, he chose one just to get out of the boutique.

"We don't have long before cocktails and dinner," Fernando said as they entered his suite, "I want a nap first, but it's probably better to shower beforehand. Get undressed."

Contessa's mouth fell open when she heard him deliver the cool instruction. "Why?" she questioned, propping a hand on her hip.

"Because I don't trust you to stay here while I shower."

County couldn't hide the guilty flash in her gaze.

"And save the humiliation speech. It only works

once." He set about removing his clothes and seemed oblivious to County's dumbfounded staring. "I'll give you a hand once I'm done here," he offered, smirking when she moved to action and raced to the bathroom for a bath sheet.

Her mouth went dry when he strolled stark naked into the bath. "Is this really necessary?" she asked, while he hummed and set the water temp in the shower. "Can't I just stay here in the bathroom while you're in there?" she bargained.

"No can do, love. I can't hear the door opening in the shower."

County stifled herself from calling that a crock. She wouldn't be surprised if the man could hear her breathing over the spray of water.

"Let's go," he prompted, watching her expectantly while he waited on her to precede him into the shower.

Realizing she had no choice, County breathed deeply and prepared to do as he said. She halted when Fernando cleared his throat.

"I don't think you'll need that," he said, his warm gaze focused on the towel she clutched. "I've seen it before, you know?" he added in an unnecessary reminder.

Hissing a soft curse, Contessa brushed the towel to the floor and stomped inside the shower.

The glass enclosed shower was spacious and tall, yet it seemed uncomfortably small when Fernando stepped inside. County discovered it wasn't the amount of space that was uncomfortable. Several times, her gaze had grown fixed on his magnificent form. Massive and cut with taut muscles, he was a specimen of what every man dreamed a gym would do for his body. The broad chest, abdomen cut like a rigid six-pack, and the breathtaking extent of his sex pulled more than a few unexpected moans from her lips.

Fernando went about his showering and was even kind enough to pass Contessa the shower gel she'd brought into the bathroom. When she began to use it, the scent of lavender teased his nostrils unexpectedly and rendered his hands weakened by need.

"You're too damn big to be sharing a shower," County grumbled, angry with herself at being too lust-driven to keep her eyes off him. "This is ridiculous," she added.

Fernando rolled his eyes and held his head beneath the water spray. "Too bad, because we don't have another choice," he said.

County decided not to argue or satisfy herself by ramming his head into the black tiled shower wall. Instead, she concentrated on lathering herself in the scented gel.

Fernando was now the one tortured by sight and felt his already stiff manhood swelling even more. He tried not to gawk, but looking away from her was next to hopeless. Watching the creamy white foam sliding across her curvaceous honey-toned frame was almost as satisfying as touch.

Almost, but not even close, he thought while stroking his hair roughened jaw and the tight muscles in his neck. Soon, his need was at full attention and he had no choice but to keep his back to her.

"To hell with this," he muttered finally, frustrated by painfully swollen desire and desperate to do something about it.

County gasped when he turned suddenly and crowded her against the back of the shower. As angered as she was by the chain of events, she had no thoughts of resisting anything he had in mind. Her lips parted, aching for his kiss. She moaned unashamed when his tongue thrust repeatedly and deeper each time. One of his hands cupped her breast while the other settled to the back of her head to keep her in place as he explored every inch of her mouth.

Moans and soft cries of need filtered over the sound of water hitting the tiles and glass of the shower. County arched herself upon him, hungry for the taste and feel of him as her arms encircled his neck. She whispered a scandalous taunt to drive him on, but Fernando needed no encouragements. He filled his big hands with her round bottom and lifted her progressively higher against the wall. His mouth trailed her neck, down to her breasts, his nose encircled her firm nipples, and he chuckled when she brushed them across his mouth in an unspoken plea for more attention.

Contessa barely noticed she was being lifted higher, until she was sitting on his broad shoulders. Her legs draped across his back and the part of her that was aching and wet for him was in direct alignment with his gorgeous face.

Fernando held her there trapped between himself and the glistening black tiles. His hands curved around her thighs—locking them in his firm grip as he helped himself to the taste of her body.

County couldn't move, completely overcome by his strength and power. Her eyes wouldn't stay open and she bucked softly against him, overcome by the feel of his tongue penetrating her femininity with such sweet, rotating lunges. She cried his name repeatedly feeling a rush of moisture stream forward as an orgasm hit her hard and fast. He didn't stop, only drinking in the proof of her satisfaction as he pleasured her even more eagerly.

Splaying her hands above her head, County flexed her inner walls around his tongue and literally cried when she climaxed more powerfully the second time. Fernando uttered a ragged groan inside her, before dragging the erotic kiss across her thighs.

They were both thoroughly weakened by unsatisfied desire. Fernando uttered a curse and pulled her down from the wall and into his arms. Kissing her savagely he left the shower running and carried her out of the bath. Stopping near the nightstand, he tore through his black leather valise until his fingers closed over a packaged condom. Still kissing heatedly, he set Contessa to her feet and went about putting protection in place.

County tried to help, but could do little more than caress the silk over steel length when her fingers grazed his swollen sex. Curving his hands around her thighs as he'd done in the shower, Fernando lifted her against the doorjamb and thrust upward. County held onto his shoulders, her nails digging into the flawless caramel skin that glistened with sweat and steam. She angled her neck to give his seeking lips more room to explore. A jolt of power surged through her when she heard the helpless grunts of pleasure he voiced just below her ear.

A steady stream of her moisture engulfed his manhood, increasing his penetration. Fernando prayed he wouldn't lose the ability to stand. Contessa was draining his strength and replacing it with an abundance of desire. His thrusts grew faster and more heated and almost frenzied in their intensity. Several times he asked if she was okay—if he was too much. Contessa's lusty cries in response brought arrogant smiles of confidence to his lips.

County moaned her disappointment, locking her legs around his back when he pulled her from the door. It was off to the king-sized four-poster bed shielded by gauzy white drapes. They practically fainted from exhaustion when they fell upon the beautiful coverings.

Their lovemaking was far from finished and Contessa reveled in everything Fernando did to her. In the midst of it all though, she couldn't help but feel that he'd been making love to her as though he might never do it again.

The cocktail party held before that evening's dinner was in gear by the time Fernando and Contessa arrived.

"Welcome!" Cufi greeted, taking Fernando's hand in a firm shake while appraising Contessa in the airy blouson dress with an uneven hem that played around her shapely calves and hugged her alluring frame. "My compliments, Mr. Simons, the lady looks very relaxed."

Fernando turned a leering gaze toward Contessa as well. "When I break 'em in, I do it right," he said, joining in when Cufi laughed at the remark and the fire in Contessa's eyes.

"A man who takes pride in his work," Cufi commended, slapping Fernando's back when a serious look crept into his eyes. "Now, we have business to discuss my friend. I had hoped to present the idea to both you and Mr. Frinks, but he never arrived."

"Cold feet?" Fernando guessed, already knowing the answer.

Cufi shrugged. "I suppose, but it's his loss. May we take a few moments?" he asked, waving his hand.

"She'll be fine," he added, noticing the look exchanged between Fernando and Contessa. "I promise you, no one will touch her. Everyone here knows she's yours."

Fernando was still on edge about going, but he finally tugged on the cuffs of his midnight blue suit coat and followed Cufi from the elegant candlelit dining room.

County's lashes fluttered then and she celebrated their departure. Focusing on the situation at hand, she honed in on one of the only women that appeared to be alone in the room.

"Incredible place, huh?" she asked the woman and prayed she could put her celebrated skills of conversation to good use.

"Yeah…" the girl drawled, absently bobbing her head to the beat of the house music that throbbed in the air. She couldn't have been more than eighteen and was clearly in an induced state, but flashed Contessa a bright smile upon answering the question.

"Been here before?" County asked, gazing around the room as though she really wasn't over-enthused by the girl's response.

"No, it's my first job, but it'll be great preparation for my acting career," she said, slapping her hands to what little material made up the skimpy white shorts she wore. "Cufi promised to help me get started," she added.

"Mmm, he must have lots of connections?" County inquired lightly.

The girl's eyes widened. "*Money* and contacts, that's what it takes. And lots of exposure. Cufi promised lots of that."

County rolled her eyes. "I'll bet."

"Did you know that he owns a villa in Nice? That's where I'll be staying, can you believe it?"

"Is that where you'll be filming?" County asked.

The girl popped her chewing gum and gave a quick toss of her blond locks. "I'm not real clear on that. Cufi's being so secretive," she laughed. "I think he wants to surprise me."

County really didn't need to hear more. Clearly, this was just as Spivey said it was. She felt sick inside.

"Here's that drink."

County and the young girl turned to find a petite round woman watching them with suspicion in her eyes and a wine cooler in her hand.

"Thanks Jessie. Oh! This is Jessie," she told Contessa and then began to enjoy her drink.

"Well, I better go find my man," County explained quickly, pumping Jessie's hand in a quick shake and hurrying off before any questions were asked.

Fernando felt even sicker following his discussion with Cufi. He decided that his first order of business would be to contact Jeff Carnes and get rid of his piece of the cursed ship. His agitation mounted further when Contessa wasn't where he'd left her. Before he completely lost his composure, he found her on a secluded area along the deck outside the living room. He walked right up behind her, took her hips in a possessive hold and pulled her back against him.

"Let's dance," he suggested.

Whirling around, County landed a cracking slap to the side of his face. "Son of a bitch," she hissed.

Grabbing her wrist, Fernando jerked her close. "Dammit, are you crazy?" he whispered.

Contessa pounded her fist against the front of the plum shirt beneath his suit coat. "I'm not afraid of you or your deranged friends. Promising young girls fame and fortune as a ruse to trap them into a life on their backs? The girl I talked to couldn't have been more than eighteen." She fixed him with a scathing look. "I'm pretty sure there're some even younger."

"Then knowing what kind of people these are should encourage you to keep it together," he advised.

"Go to hell, I'm not afraid of them or you."

"Hell, County do you think who you are is going to keep you safe?" he asked, tempted to shake her into acknowledging the danger of the situation.

"Who *I* am?" Contessa breathed, shaking her head in disgust. "Let's talk about who *you* are, Fernando Ramsey? A shameful bastard making money off the rape of young girls. And here you've got everyone fooled into thinking your father's the bad guy when it's you and your sick friends."

"County—"

"No. Let me tell you something," she said, slamming her fist against his chest again, "you forget everything about me. Forget we ever met. I don't want to hear from you. I don't want to hear anything you have to say."

The hate oozed from her voice and her eyes like daggers and Fernando didn't like it. His grip had weakened around her wrist and County used the opportunity to wrench herself free and turn her back on him.

He knew he could get her to listen later, Fernando assured himself. It was now that frightened him. Hearing her say how much she despised him was almost too much.

"Just like your father and murdering uncle," she muttered, staring out over the moonlit ocean. "But I think you're worse Fernando—to condemn a woman to a life like this? How many have there been?" she inquired absently, her expression clearing suddenly. "And I let myself fall in love with you," she admitted and then grimaced, "in lust is probably more accurate. You're a man who thinks woman are prizes, objects for the pleasure of men." She turned to face him. "I should've seen that so long ago. After all, you *do* own a strip club."

Fernando bounded toward her and Contessa straightened, readying herself for another heated verbal exchanged. Bracing his hands along either side of her against the railing, he bent to look directly into her eyes.

"You're so very wrong about me," his deep voice rumbled and matched the depth of emotion in his heavenly light brown eyes.

"Yes, I was, wasn't I?" she reciprocated.

Fernando blinked at the defeated tone in her voice.

"Dinner is served!"

Each thankful for the interruption, Contessa allowed Fernando to lead her from the deck.

When they were gone, Jessie, Cufi Muhammad's personal assistant, emerged from the shadows.

The delicious-looking dinner of Cornish hen, pecan dressing, steamed spinach and pumpernickel rolls had a nauseating effect on Contessa. She didn't even pretend to have an appetite and many of the feasting guests noticed.

"I think she'll be happier in bed!" Fernando remarked, rousing a roar of laughter from the long candlelit table. He excused them and quickly escorted County back to his cabin.

Inside the suite, County wanted to mentally block all visions of her time spent there with Fernando. Of course, that was impossible when they'd made love in every corner of the place. Made love, she thought, made sex was a more precise observation in her mind—regardless of what her heart said.

"Do you need help out of this?" Fernando asked, trailing his fingers along the bodice of her dress.

County flinched and jerked away from him. Seconds later, she disappeared into the bathroom.

Fernando stood debating on whether to go after her, when his cell phone rang. "Yeah?" he snapped into the receiver.

"It's me."

"Moses? What's up?" he asked, only absently wondering why his brother was calling.

"Have you seen any of the girls from the club?"

"Not a one," Fernando sighed.

"Well, your time's up. You need to get out of there and quick."

Looking away from the bathroom door, Fernando frowned. "I just got here. Ship hasn't even set sail yet."

"Which is a good thing. Your cover's blown."

"What? How the hell could you know that?"

"You'll never believe me, so I'll explain the particulars later. Right now, you need to up and get your ass outta there."

Fernando raked a hand through his hair. "That's not easy man. Contessa's here."

"I know."

"And you'll explain later?" Fernando guessed,

too on edge to question further. "She doesn't trust me, Mo—thinks I'm in business with these fools. I'll never get her to leave willingly."

"Then you'll have to make her."

"How? Go knock her out?"

"Exactly."

"Mo—"

"There's chloroform and a rag in the nightstand drawer. Use it."

"How—"

"Just do it, man! Save the questions for later. Get County and get to the starboard deck. Now!"

Fernando slammed the phone shut, located the chloroform and the rag and headed for the bathroom. At the door, he closed his eyes. "Lord, please don't let her kill me for this," he prayed, and then uttered a relieved sigh that she hadn't locked the door.

Cufi Muhammad sat in his office. He was joined by several of his men and Jessie Stevens who supervised the women aboard the ship.

"Now tell me again and slowly Jessie. You're sure of this?"

"I heard them talking."

"And she said his name was—"

"Ramsey. Fernando Ramsey."

Silence filled the office for a long while, and then came the sound of Cufi's fist hitting the desk.

"Should I go after them?" Carlos McPhereson asked his boss.

Cufi lifted a hand and shook his head. "Wait until we set sail in the morning. We'll get rid of them once we're at sea." He reached for the phone. After a few moments, he spoke into the receiver. "What the hell is your son doing on my ship, Marcus?"

Contessa woke with a languid stretch across the crisp forest green bed linens. She took a moment to open her eyes and as they adjusted to her unfamiliar surroundings, she wrinkled her brow and tried her best to remember how she got there. Wherever *there* was, it wasn't the last place she recalled being. Then, she realized that she was half naked beneath the sheets.

"I didn't think you'd want to sleep in that dress."

The rough voice sent her anger soaring. She turned to see Fernando leaning against one of the bedposts. He was fully dressed, a fact she took mild comfort in. Still, it did nothing to stop her from trying to bolt from the bed.

Anticipating her move, Fernando caught her easily. They tussled for a while, the sheet twisting around her body did nothing to help County achieve her goal of escaping. He was pinning her to the bed, his fingers interlaced between hers as he pressed them down. His big hard frame almost cut off her circulation, but still she struggled.

"Listen to me," he urged, unmindful of her flailing legs as he rested between them.

County managed to free one hand and landed a vicious blow to his cheek. "Jackass! Son of a bitch— get off me! Get off I said!"

Pinning her free hand back to the tangled linens, he pressed his mouth to her ear. "You're wrong, you're wrong about me, you're wrong," he chanted, feeling her heaving breasts slow their exertions as she quieted.

"Where am I?" she breathed.

"A hotel in Kauai."

"How?"

"Moses."

Blinking and searching his eyes when he looked down at her, she couldn't even think of what to ask next.

"Moses called when we got back to the cabin last night. He told me they were on to us. I'm not working with Cufi Muhammad." He swore, feeling her stiffen beneath him once again. "I was trying to get evidence against my father. I knew he was involved in something shady, but I had no idea it was anything like this. I had to see it for myself," he said and then quieted before moving off her.

Contessa was still for a minute, before rising slowly from the bed. She kept the sheet folded tightly around her. Fernando watched her move to an armchair with the coverings bunched around her body. He felt his chest tighten with uncertainty and fear of what she might say.

"I'm sorry, sorry I doubted you." She spoke in a whisper, her brown eyes wide and staring blankly into the distance. "To think you really could've been involved in something like that."

Fernando left the bed and knelt before her. "Don't do that," he ordered, catching portions of the sheet in his hands. "It's not necessary. You had every right to think what you did. At least I know I played a convincing role." He smiled encouragingly. "At least that's what I *thought*," he added, his smile fading a bit.

"How'd Moses know we were in danger?" County asked.

Fernando shook his head. "I have no idea, but I intend to find out," he swore.

"What about the girls?" she whispered, her voice holding traces of anxiety. "They can't stay there."

"And they won't," Fernando vowed, kissing her bare shoulder. "Moses wouldn't go into how he knew we were in danger, but he's at work on this now and we'll get every last girl off that damn boat. I swear."

Relatively at ease by that news, County nodded. Again, the soft-lit room was bathed in silence while they both took stock of all that had happened within the past months.

"I guess I should be getting back," County said finally.

"To Chicago," Fernando guessed.

"It's where I belong."

You belong with me, he corrected silently. "I don't want you to leave," he chose to tell her aloud.

Contessa's eyes filled with all the emotions she'd tried desperately to mask. She scooted forward and smoothed the back of her hand across his whiskered cheek. "Fernando, I just don't know if we're ready."

"Don't," he blurted, grimacing over the fact that he'd heard more of the statement than he'd wanted to. "Don't tell me that. Don't say it's over."

"But I don't know where we go from here," she said, trying to swallow the sob rising in her throat.

Fernando cupped her face in his hands. "Do you love me?" he asked.

"I really believe I do," she said, honesty glowing in her warm gaze. "But if that were true how could I have doubted you so fast? Believed you'd be involved with something like this—if I *really* loved you?"

Fernando bowed his head, the muscle in his jaw working frantically as he fought to keep his frustration hidden. "Trust comes with love," he said, sounding as though he were telling himself. "But you have to know someone in order to trust. Even then it takes a long time to build. Maybe it hasn't been long enough for all of that to happen," he finished.

Contessa blinked, looking down at her hands blurred by her tears. "Maybe it hasn't been," she agreed quietly.

"I don't want to let you go," he said, his voice firm as he pressed his forehead to her chest.

County sniffled. "I don't want to go," she admitted, kissing the top of his head. "But we moved so fast and so many things were in the way to cloud our vision. Maybe we need to take a step back—to be sure we're going in the right direction."

"I'll buy that," he said, looking up at her then. "Just please don't say that we can't see each other."

County smiled, unable to prevent the devilish twinkle from sparkling in her eyes. "Well, that wouldn't be any fun, would it?"

"Hell, no," he agreed, bowing low to kiss her knee where it peeked out from beneath the sheet. "I never want to lose you," he spoke against her skin and then fixed her with his striking eyes. "I've never known a woman to match me word for word, play for play—who can satisfy me physically so much that I find myself wondering what we'd be like together after twenty years."

County's lips parted and she sat a little straighter.

"I don't want to lose any of that," he went on, "so if it's time you need, then that's fine with me because time is all I want with you."

His words—so sweet, so dear and so heartfelt, rendered her speechless. Sniffing softly, she leaned down to place a tender kiss to his mouth. He reciprocated by pulling her close to cradle her in his arms. Drowsiness weighed her eyelids once more.

Contessa fell asleep praying that Fernando's embrace would belong to her always.

"Any word from the guys?" Moses Ramsey asked as he and his captain exited the elevator.

Carlos McPhereson shook his head, while extracting the razor-slim cellular from his pocket. "They're sittin' tight 'til the authorities get there. They'll call once the boat is secure," he said.

Moses nodded, his dark gaze focused straight ahead as they headed down the hotel corridor.

Suddenly, Carlos's steps slowed and he fixed his boss with a probing look.

"What?" Moses asked, stopping a few feet ahead of Carlos.

"Man, do you think we got enough this time? Enough to put that son of a bitch Cufi under the jail?"

Moses bowed his head and sighed. "I pray we do 'Los. But even still, we gotta risk it."

Carlos began to rub his massive hands together while grimacing at Moses's summation. "I hate like hell goin' full throttle out there and wasting years of work," he confided.

An apologetic smile softened Moses's dark, handsome face. "I hate it too, kid. But we've already unzipped our fly here. No turnin' back now, I'm afraid."

"You and I both know that it can be risky getting

evidence found on the open seas to stick," Carlos mentioned.

Moses offered no response. Carlos was right. They'd both hoped their longtime surveillance of *The Wind Rage* would've produced hard evidence: land-based property, paperwork—something concrete that Cufi Muhammad and his partners couldn't weasel out of. Unfortunately, neither Carlos nor the rest of the men in place had ever been farther than the ship.

"Listen man," Moses said, stepping closer to clap a hand to Carlos's shoulder. "I couldn't have asked for a better job to be done on this. You should be proud. We're gonna get these fools and you're gonna get your life back."

Carlos's green eyes twinkled with devilish light. "Hell man, are you kidding? You know hunting down crazed maniacs is my life."

Moses's grin wasn't humor-filled. "No. That would be *my* life."

Carlos's laughter died on his tongue as he took in the underlying meaning of his friend's statement.

"How is she?"

"She's fine," Carlos responded without hesitation, knowing who *she* was without hearing a name. "But you can go see that for yourself."

Moses smoothed one hand across his bald head. "You know why I can't do that," he grumbled.

"Because you're not ready to tell her the truth."

"No. Because she's *still* better off away from me."

"Mo—"

"'Los? That's the end of it, all right?" Moses asked, though he actually required no response.

Carlos let the subject drop and followed Moses on down the silent hall towards Fernando Ramsey's hotel suite.

County left the bathroom feeling no better than she had before she'd gone in. She'd hoped a splash of cool water upon her face would leave her feeling refreshed and less edgy. It hadn't. There was only one thing that would do that: knowing Cufi Muhammad and his ship of perversions was a thing of the past.

Across the room, Fernando sat in the armchair near the window. He watched her for several moments once she'd left the bathroom. Unfortunately, her expression offered no clues to her mood.

"Hungry?" he called, seeing her jump when his voice reached her ears.

Wringing her hands, County shook her head and ventured slowly from the bathroom door. "I don't think I could keep anything down," she admitted, tightening the belt around the comfy terry robe she wore.

"Sit with me?" Fernando asked, praying she'd not turn away from his closeness. He hid his smile when she showed no hesitation in closing the distance between them.

County cuddled against Fernando, resting her head against his shoulder. She relished the feel of contentment that radiated through his powerful form and seeped into her weary body. The events of that night seemed as though they'd happened a lifetime ago and she shuddered at the gross inaccuracy of the statement.

"Hey?" Fernando whispered, rubbing his hands across her back. "It's all right, it's over," he said, hugging her close as her trembling intensified.

"Is—is it?" County chattered out. "I have the most awful feeling that they'll get away. It's like the Ramseys can do anything—get away with anything."

Fernando ignored the painful stab her words sent through his heart. He couldn't help but agree with her.

"When will you go back to Chicago?" he asked, deciding to broach the subject and get it over with.

County's shivering ceased a bit. "Soon. I think it's best."

The painful stabbing in Fernando's heart grew stronger. "When can I see you?" he asked.

"It's hard to say," she replied, forcing a light tone to her voice. "There's so much I need to catch up—"

"When can I be with you?"

County breathed a relieved sigh when a heavy knock landed on the room door. The loaded question went unanswered.

Fernando pressed a kiss to County's head and went to answer the door. He nodded and stepped aside to allow his brother and Carlos entrance to the room. Moses went right over to Contessa and planted a soft kiss to her forehead before introducing her to Carlos.

"Are the girls safe?" County asked, searching Moses's intense, narrow stare.

"We're expecting a call about that any minute," he assured her.

"How good are the chances that they'll pay for what they've done?" she asked, curling her fingers around the lapels of the denim jacket he wore.

Moses flashed a quick look toward Carlos before smiling down at County. "That *will* happen—you have my word."

The sound of a cell phone pierced the air a second later.

County turned away, while Moses handled the call. She, Fernando and Carlos were just indulging in a bit of idle chatter when Moses's roar silenced them.

"Idiots!" he raged. "Are they sure?… Dammit how the hell long did it take them to get there?"

Carlos, Fernando and County stared wide-eyed as Moses ended the call.

"The ship was empty."

The simple statement helped to maintain the silence for several more seconds. Eventually, the reality of the words hit home.

"How?" Carlos asked.

Moses shrugged, while shoving the cellular into

his pocket. "When they stormed the ship it was empty. No passengers, no crew, nothing."

"But weren't they watching the ship until the police arrived?" Contessa wanted to know.

Nodding, Moses leaned against the message desk. "My guys saw no one leave. They haven't got a clue."

"Son of a bitch!" Fernando raged, pounding a massive fist against the wall he stood closest to.

Moses nodded toward Carlos and the two made silent decisions to leave then.

"We'll call once we get back to the ship, let you know what we find." Moses told his brother.

County saw the men out of the suite, then closed her eyes and rested her forehead against the door. A crashing sound caused her to whirl around a moment later. Her eyes widened once more at the sight of an overturned table courtesy of Fernando.

"You've got to calm down," she urged, taking slow cautious steps toward him. "This won't solve a damn thing, you know?"

Fernando slanted her a frosty glance and raised his hand. "All I know is you're right to want to get as far away as possible from me and my damn screwed up family."

"Fern—"

"No, Contessa," he ordered, shaking his head as he turned his back toward her. "Hell you pretty much predicted this crap would happen."

County smoothed her hands across the sleeves of the ankle-length terry robe. "I was just talking," she murmured.

"You were still right. The Ramseys get away with anything."

"Fernando, I wasn't including you in that. Hell, I shouldn't have even said it. Cufi Muhammad had those girls, not your family."

"You forget my father, County," Fernando whispered, fixing her with his steady transluscent stare. "Marc Ramsey—the one who provides that fool with all his *feisty* Americans."

County shook her head while moving closer. "This wasn't your fault. What *your father* did wasn't *your* fault. I won't let you blame yourself for this especially when you've been so determined to get to the bottom of it." She stopped right before Fernando and caught the collar of his shirt in her hands. "If you hadn't delved so deep this never would've been discovered."

Fernando didn't seem impressed. "*You* discovered it," he reminded her.

County's smile was pure wickedness. "Well…" she drawled. "That's because *I'm* Contessa Warren."

"And I don't want to let you go," he said, his stern expression softening a bit.

"And I don't want you to."

Fernando's gaze faltered. "Maybe you should."

"But I don't," she argued, moving closer, "you

should know by now Ramsey that I always get what I want."

"Don't play with me County," he warned, encircling her body in his steely embrace. "Now is definitely not the time to say things to me you don't mean."

"I don't want you to let me go," she reiterated, searching his face with her luminous stare. "I want this. I want us."

"When can I see you?" he asked, restating his earlier question.

"Anytime," County replied without hesitation.

The adorable eye-crinkling grin appeared. "When can I be with you again?" he asked.

County curved her arms about his neck and grazed her teeth across his earlobe. "Now," she whispered, laughing when Fernando lifted her in his arms and carried her back to bed.

Everybody's guilty of something…

ONE NIGHT WITH YOU

National bestselling author

Gwynne Forster

Determined to restore his reputation after
losing a bitter court battle, Reid Maguire needs
Judge Kendra Rutherford to set things right.
But the sexy judge is making it hard for him to
keep his priorities straight—and soon they're
both guilty of losing their hearts….

"Like fine wine, Gwynne Forster's
storytelling skills get better over time."
—*Essence* bestselling author Donna Hill

*Available the first week of March,
wherever books are sold.*

KIMANI™
ROMANCE

National bestselling author
FRANCINE CRAFT

The Way You Make Me Feel

The diva who had amnesia…

Suffering from amnesia, singer Stevie Simms
finds refuge in Damien Steele's home. As they
become lovers, Damien's frozen heart thaws
and Steve starts to recover. But someone is
trying to kill Stevie—if only she could
remember who!

*Available the first week of March,
wherever books are sold.*

KIMANI™
ROMANCE

KPFC0090307

"Robyn Amos dishes up a fast-paced, delectable love story…!"
—*Romantic Times BOOKreviews*

BESTSELLING AUTHOR

AMOS ROBYN

Promise ME

After taking a break from a demanding career and a controlling fiancé, Cara Williams was ready to return to her niche in the computer field. It looked like clear sailing—until AJ Gray came on the scene. As the powerful president of Captial Computer Consulting, AJ offered Cara the expertise she needed—even as his kisses triggered her worst fears and her deepest desires.

Coming the first week of March,
wherever books are sold.

ARABESQUE®

www.kimanipress.com

KPRA0070307

An emotional story of family and forgiveness...

National bestselling author

PHILLIP THOMAS DUCK

PLAYING WITH
DESTINY

As brothers, Colin and Courtney Sheffield know
their lives will always be connected. But their mistakes,
and those of their absent father before them, have tangled
them in a web of bitterness and regret neither can shake.

As painful secrets threaten to shatter their futures,
both must deal with the emotional complexities
of true brotherhood.

"Duck writes with a voice that is unique,
entertaining and compelling."
—Robert Fleming, author of *Havoc After Dark*

*Available the first week of March,
wherever books are sold.*

www.kimanipress.com KPPTD0390307

Second chance for romance…

When
Valentines
Collide

Award-winning author
ADRIANNE
*B*YRD

Therapists Chante and Michael Valentine agree to a "sex-
therapy" retreat to save their marriage. At first the seminar
revives their passion—but their second chance at love is
threatened when a devastating secret is revealed.

"Byrd proves again that she's a wonderful storyteller."
—*Romantic Times BOOKreviews* on *The Beautiful Ones*

Available the first week of February,
wherever books are sold.

KIMANI™
ROMANCE

www.kimanipress.com

KPAB0050207